Also by Sarah Darer Littman

SARAH DARER LITTMAN

IN CASE YOU MISSED IT

Scholastic Inc.

10 9 8 7 6 5 4 3 2 1   16 17 18 19 20

Printed in the U.S.A.   40

First printing 2016
Book design by Nina Goffi

*Dedicated to the memory of my beloved mother,
Susan Silverstone Darer, who was taken from us suddenly
and unexpectedly four days after the sale of this book.
If I can be half as wonderful a woman as she was,
I will have lived a good life.*

ONE

It's possible that there are more irrational, irritating parents on the planet than mine, but if you ask me what the probability of that is at this particular moment, I'd say it's zero.

My friend Margo's dad scored tickets for an all-ages Einstein's Encounter show at the Bowery Ballroom in two weeks because his company does accounting for someone or something. My parents said I can't go because there's no parental chaperone.

Never mind that I'm sixteen, taking my driving test in three weeks, and have gotten practically straight As (only three A-minuses and a B-plus) since I started high school. I'm like a poster child for responsibility.

"Why not?" I ask them.

"Because it's dangerous," my mom says. "Didn't you hear about those kids who died at Electric Zoo?"

"Ugh. But that was electronic music," I reply. My parents

look at me blankly. Clearly they don't get it. I point out that those kids were going for the drugs *and* the music, and I'm just going for the music. And what I don't say is: also, because I'm in love with the lead singer, Davy Linklater. The fact that he's already married is a minor detail.

"I'm sure they told their parents they were going for the music, too," my dad says.

Apparently, my parents think I'm a lying druggie, despite the fact that I've never given them any evidence for that. So they refused to let me go unless a parent comes along. But Margo's dad only got us three tickets. Uggggggghhhhhh!

"So what you're saying is that you don't trust me," I say to them. God, even I can hear how much a cliché I sound like. But seriously?

And then my mom actually utters these words in reply: "We *do* trust you, Sammy. It's everyone else we don't trust."

What does that even *mean*? Am I supposed to live in a bubble for the rest of my life because they don't trust everyone else?

"I'm going to college the year after next. Are you planning to send me to college with a chaperone, too?" I ask, exasperated.

"Don't be ridiculous, Sammy!" my mom snaps.

"*I'm* the one being ridiculous?"

Then my dad steps in and says, "Stop being rude to your mother," before sending me to my room.

Another fun night at Casa Wallach.

"But you *have* to come!" Margo says at lunch the next day, flicking her red-gold hair off her shoulders. "It's going to be *epic*."

"Tell me something I *don't* know," I groan.

"Tell them you're having a sleepover at my house," suggests Rosa, my best friend since first grade.

"My parents might be totally unreasonable, but they aren't *stupid*," I remind her. "I ask to go to a concert, they say no, and then I say I'm having a sleepover at your house? Helene will be on the phone to your mom before I finish the sentence."

Both Rosa and Margo have to admit that I have a point there. They know what freaks Dick and Helene can be.

I sit in miserable contemplative silence, playing with my dark-chocolate-covered raisins. There's got to be a solution. I want to go so badly I can taste it.

"What about . . . if you said you were having a study sleepover . . . for APs or something," Rosa says slowly, fixing her dark brown eyes on me, thoughtfully. "At someone's house that they don't know that well?"

"Yeah, but really you could come to the concert and sleep over at my house!" Margo exclaims.

My parents are so obsessed with me doing well on APs, they might actually buy that. I feel a tiny flicker of hope that maybe, just maybe, this could work.

"I'll ask Mom before SAT prep tonight," I say.

"She has to say yes," Rosa says. "*Las tres amigas* need to go to this concert together!"

As I head to AP Stats, I see Jamie Moss standing at the end of the hall, leaning up against a locker, looking totally hot, as usual. His dark hair hangs below his collar because it's lacrosse season and he's got to have the right lax flow. (His words, not mine. But hard to disagree.) Meanwhile, his muscles are set off to perfection by his Brooklawne Blue Devils T-shirt.

Unfortunately, he's talking to Geneva Grady, who according to popular opinion is considered to be pretty hot. I guess she is if you like blond-haired, blue-eyed, super-skinny girls who hang on your every word if you're a guy, but ignore you if you're a girl.

I will seriously die if he likes *her*.

It's no secret that Geneva likes *him*. She keeps touching his arm every thirty seconds, like she owns him, when they're not even dating. I would have heard.

Plus, the minute he sees me, he pulls his oh-so-hot body off the locker and says, "Hey, Sammy, what's up?" with the cutest grin.

Forget solar panels. His smile is a legit alternative energy source.

If looks could kill, however, I'd be six feet under after the one Geneva just shot me.

"Nothing much," I say, flashing Jamie my brightest smile, which admittedly is many lumens dimmer than his.

"Hey, Geneva, I'll see you in class," he tells her, in obvious dismissal.

She doesn't take it well, turning on her heel and marching away, with a parting death glare at me.

Too bad. I'm basking in Jamie's undivided attention, which wraps me in a cocoon of warmth and reassurance. At least until he asks: "So, Sammy, do you have last night's homework? The lacrosse game ran late and I didn't get to finish it."

It's at times like this I worry that Jamie only likes me for my brains, which is ironic because I'm supposed to want him to do that, right? But I want him to like me for being a girl, too. I can't see him inviting me to the prom solely on the basis of my amazing math skills.

Reluctantly, I take my homework out of my backpack and hand it to him so he can copy my answers.

"Did you win?" I ask.

"What?" He's busy copying all my hard-figured problems onto his blank paper. He didn't even start his homework, much less not finish.

"Did you win the game?"

"Oh yeah," he says, copying furiously. "We killed them, five to one."

He actually stops for a moment and looks at me. His

eyes. They're like gazing into a midsummer sky on a perfect beach day.

"You should have come to the game," he says. "It was at home."

"I couldn't . . ." I have to look away because I'm embarrassed, suddenly, by how nerdy what I'm going to say next will sound. "I had a Lighthouse Book Club meeting."

"I can't believe you go to a club to read more books," he says, going back to copying. "I can barely get through the ones I have to read for school."

"But these are fun books," I say. "And it's not like we have to analyze them to death for symbolism or write five-page essays like for class."

"Come to the game next time," he says. "Where's your school spirit?"

I swallow the question that nearly escapes: *Where's the rule that says my school spirit is defined by attendance at sporting events?*

I have a funny feeling that's not the kind of speech that will encourage a date to the prom.

Instead, I mutter, "Maybe. Let me know when you've got another home game."

Jamie flashes me one more adorable grin and hands me back my homework. "Sure thing," he says. "And thanks. I get kicked off the team if I don't keep my grades up."

So why don't you do your homework? I wonder, as we walk into class together.

But the strange, smug feeling I get from the annoyed look on Geneva Grady's face pushes that thought from my mind.

I bring up the sleepover idea to Mom as we're getting in the car to go to SAT prep after school. The sleepover host was carefully chosen—Kate Pierce, a girl in my AP Gov class who I've mentioned several times in conversation. Her name is familiar to my parents, but not so familiar that they know her parents well enough to call them.

"We're going to study and then watch a movie for a break," I tell her. "But we can quiz each other on the questions."

"Okay," Mom says, buckling her seat belt. "Did you adjust your mirrors?"

There's a 100 percent probability that my mom wasn't fully listening to what I just said. But who cares. She said okay.

I check the mirrors, start the car, and put it in drive. It's so much more relaxing to practice driving with Dad because he's checking his phone half the time. Mom is a hypervigilant driving hawk. Just feeling her tension makes me more nervous.

Switching on the radio to help me relax, I pull out of the driveway.

"I didn't see you look in both directions," Mom says.

I totally did. My mom has apparently forgotten that humans have peripheral vision. But I don't want to start this joyride off with a fight.

When I get to the stop sign at the end of the street, I turn my head so exaggeratedly to make Mom happy that I end up giving myself a crick in the right side of my neck. That'll teach me.

"Dad's going to be home late again tonight." Mom sighs. "It's those protesters again."

My dad is the CEO of New Territories Bank Corporation, which has been targeted by protesters for the last two weeks. They're upset about the bank's role in the mortgage crisis and housing slump or something, so they've set up camp outside my dad's office in New York City.

Meanwhile, their protest is leading to *more* protests from the local residents and businesses who are annoyed by the disruption. It's giving Dad headaches galore. The fact that it's all that he talks about at the moment gives *me* headaches galore.

"He's home late all the time," I point out. "Why is tonight different from all other nights?"

My mom ignores my question. "I'm starting to feel like a single parent," she says. "I have a job, too, in case anyone's forgotten."

Mom also used to be in banking, but after she had my

brother, RJ, she decided to start her own consulting business helping small businesses so she could be around more. Or that's what she thought, anyway. Basically, she just works a lot more hours at home instead of having to commute into the city.

"We haven't forgotten," I say. "What's up with that new ice-cream store?"

"Lickety Splits," she says. "The grand opening is on Sunday."

"Cool. Are they giving out free ice cream?"

"Move left!" Mom says sharply, clutching the door handle. "You almost took off that wing mirror!"

I turn the wheel toward the center line.

"SAMMY! Stay in your lane!"

"Make up your mind," I mutter, edging the wheel slightly back to the right.

"Are you even paying attention to what you're doing?" Mom says, switching off the radio.

"Why'd you turn off the radio?" I complain. "Music helps keep me relaxed."

"You're a little *too* relaxed," Mom snaps. "You need to stay focused."

When Mom's in the car with me, I'm more frazzled than focused. I need music to distract me from the nervous tension that emits from her like nuclear radiation. Now that she's turned off the radio, I'm zapped with the full force of it. I end up gripping the steering wheel so tight it makes my knuckles white, even though my driving instructor told me specifically I shouldn't do that.

"So what about Dad?" I ask, trying to get her off the topic of my driving.

"It seems like things are heating up and—STOP SIGN!"

"I KNOW!" I shout back. "I was braking, in case you didn't notice, which obviously you didn't because you were too busy YELLING AT ME."

"You weren't braking hard enough," Mom says. "You have to stop at the white line, not over it."

I look out the window. I'm maybe one inch over the white line, if that.

"Seriously? That's margin of error."

"Is that what you're going to tell the DMV examiner when you fail your road test?" Mom demands.

The car behind me honks. I've been so busy arguing with Mom that I forgot to go.

Flustered, I put my foot down on the gas a little too hard and the car accelerates with a screech of burning rubber.

"Slow down!" Mom yelps. "You're supposed to be driving, not drag racing."

I'm desperate to get my license, but I'm beginning to wonder if having my mom criticize me the entire way to SAT prep is worth it. Like I'm not stressed out enough about having to take the SAT in just over a month, on top of worrying about passing my driving test, taking four AP exams, and wondering if Jamie Moss will ask me to prom.

But driving means freedom. It means that this summer, when all the Very Important Tests are over, I might actually be able to get a job *and* have a social life, without being dependent on my parents' willingness to take me from point A to point B. Without having to listen to their awful music, lectures, or corny jokes while trapped in a moving box on wheels.

Not to mention their constant criticism.

"Sammy, you haven't looked in your rearview mirror once since the stop sign. They put them in cars for a reason, you know."

"I was making sure I stayed in my lane and didn't take off any wing mirrors," I retort.

"You have to be able to multitask," Mom says.

"You just told me I had to be focused. Now you're telling me to multitask. Make up your mind!"

"I don't have to let you get your license, young lady."

"Fine. Then you'll be stuck driving me everywhere all the time."

Mom opens her mouth to say something to me, but shouts, "Watch that truck pulling out!"

I slam on the brakes and narrowly miss hitting a King John's Port-O-Potties truck that totally appeared from nowhere, even though I have the right-of-way. Hitting that would really stink. Literally.

"I had the right-of-way," I protest. "I'm on the major thoroughfare, not him. It would have been his fault if we had an accident."

He doesn't seem to think so. He gives me the finger and pulls out in front of me.

"So you'll be happy that it was his fault if you end up paralyzed from the neck down?" Mom says.

And everyone says teenage girls are the drama queens.

"Of course not!" I say, following behind the truck, making sure to keep a safe stopping distance so that Mom doesn't have anything else to get on my case about. "But that's not going to happen."

"No one thinks it's going to happen," Mom says. "Even if you're the best driver in the world, you still have to look out for other drivers."

I've heard my dad say the same thing a zillion times, but somehow he manages to do it without implying I'm the worst driver. He's always pushing me to do things I'm afraid to do, like parallel parking. The problem with Dad is he gets frustrated if I don't do it perfectly on the first or second try.

I'm not sure whose sigh of relief is louder when I pull into the parking lot of Stratospheric Scores. Luckily, there's a big parking space for me to pull into, which I do with only a hissed intake of breath from my mother. I grab my SAT book from the backseat and make my escape.

"Later, Mom!" I call as I walk away from the car.

"Don't leave the car door open when you get out!" Mom yells at my retreating back. "It might scratch the paint on the car next to us!"

I pretend not to hear her and keep walking. Selective deafness to Mom's voice is a necessary survival trait.

"Hey, Sammy! Nice parking job."

Noah Woods, who's in my AP English class and Lighthouse Book Club, watched me pull in. He got his license in January. I'm so jealous.

"Are you serious or are you being sarcastic?" I ask, tilting my head.

"Serious," he says.

I breathe a sigh of relief.

"After being in the car with my mom, I'm usually convinced that I'm an Agent of Death on wheels."

Noah laughs.

"Ah yes, I remember those days well. I'm surprised my mom didn't rip the handle off the passenger door, she was clutching it so hard the entire time I was driving," he says. "It gets better when you pass your test. Trust me."

"I can't wait," I say. "I just wish I didn't have so many *other* tests to think about at the same time."

"Yeah, this year is brutal," Noah says. "Only two and a half more months to go."

"Two and a half more months with all those Very Important Tests." I sigh.

"Hang in there," Noah says. "We'll get through it."

Over Noah's shoulder, I spot Rosa and her wavy chocolate-colored bob waiting for me in the lobby, waving at me to hurry and join her.

"See you inside," I tell Noah, and despite feeling a little rude, I run on ahead.

"So? What happened?" Rosa asks.

"She said yes. Well, to the AP sleepover, not the concert."

"But that means you can come to the concert, right?"

"If we can figure out the carpool situation, yeah."

"Yes!" Rosa says, high-fiving me. "This is going to be awesome! Have you told Margo yet?"

"Not yet. I was *driving*. With *Helene*. You know how that stresses me out."

"Gotcha. *No problemo, mi hermana*. I'll do it."

She sends a group text to Margo and me, and instructs Margo to try to figure out the transport stuff.

Knowing I've got the concert to look forward to gets me through the mind-numbing boringness of an hour and a half of SAT prep. I'm starting to feel like a trained test monkey. I half expect a treat to come out of the computer when I get the right answer and an electric shock when I get a wrong one. I get so fed up and bored with being on the hamster wheel of testing that sometimes I just want to pick any old answer so I can get it over with and move on to the things I really care about.

But that would be committing suicide with my future—or so I'm told at every possible opportunity. I have to do well on all these tests or I won't get into a good college. And if I don't get into a good college, then I won't get a good job, and if I don't get a good job, then I'll end up asking, "Do you want fries with that?" or "Can I supersize you?" or worse, living on the streets in a cardboard box with all of my worldly possessions in a shopping cart that I stole from Walmart.

So I sit at the computer trying to focus, even though I hate every minute.

The problem is that Margo keeps texting Rosa and me in the group chat about the Einstein's Encounter concert.

sooooooooo excited. did you listen to the new single they released today? it's awesome.

I guess Rosa is trying to focus, too, because five minutes later, there's another.

hello? are you alive?

are you guys mad at me? why aren't you answering?

HELLO?!!!!!!!!!!!!!!!!!

I get so tired of my phone buzzing that I finally text back.

no, i'm not mad and yes, i'm dead.

Rosa writes:

me too, from boredom, at SAT prep. later.

Of course, Margo has to text again to tell us she got the text and she'll talk to us when we get out, instead of you know, just stopping.

Back to stupid SAT math word problems: *Of the 80 students in class, 25 are studying Chinese, 15 French, and 13 Spanish. 3 are studying Chinese and French; 4 are studying French and Spanish; 2 are studying Chinese and Spanish; and none is studying all 3 languages at the same time. How many students are not studying any of the 3 languages?*

First of all, can you imagine the PTA freaking out if we had classes of eighty students? They'd be camping out in front of the school board, just like the protesters are doing outside my dad's job, except the PTA of our school would have designer tents with luxury King John's Port-O-Potties and takeout deliveries from expensive restaurants for dinner. Second of all, how come no one is studying Italian, or German, or Japanese? Italian sounds so romantic. And all the Anime Club kids want to learn Japanese.

Whatever. Stop thinking, Sammy, and solve the problem.

I'm so glad when class is over. I'm tired and starving, and worst of all, I still have at least three hours' worth of homework to tackle when I get home. But I've got Einstein's Encounter on the horizon. It's only because of that I don't complain when Mom tells me she's driving home because she's on her last nerve and can't cope with being a passenger while I drive. I just say, "Fine, whatever," because I want to spend the drive home texting with Rosa and Margo about concert plans.

"I'm picking up takeout on the way home," Mom says.

"Can we get sushi?"

"No, I already ordered from Mama Lucia's," Mom says. "I just want to pick up and go."

"But we always get Italian," I say, pouting. "Because that's the only thing RJ eats."

"We don't always get Italian, and please stop whining, Samantha," Mom snaps. "I'm tired, and I have a headache."

Really? You've *got a headache,* I think as I stare out the window, sulking. The truth is we *do* always order from Mama Lucia's because it's RJ's favorite. And RJ's in eighth grade and a giant pain, so my mom's just avoiding a fight with the picky eater. But she doesn't have three hours of homework to do.

RJ's playing video games when we get home, with Scruffles, our rescue mutt, curled up on the sofa next to him, at least till I walk in the door. Scruffles leaps off the couch, runs to me, and starts barking and chasing his tail in a circle. Watching him, you'd think I'd been away for a month instead of a few hours.

Just another reason why dogs are awesome, and Scruffles is the most awesome dog of all.

"Yes, I know, pupper, you missed me," I croon, scratching behind his ears. "But I'm back now!"

"He didn't realize he missed you till you walked in the door," RJ says. "Before that, he was perfectly fine."

My brother doesn't want me to have any joy in my life.

"You're not a dog mind reader," I tell him. "You have no idea what goes on in Scruffles' head."

"Neither do you," RJ says. "And based on the evidence, he was happy."

Mom's in the kitchen unloading the food. I head in and put down my backpack. Scruffles trots after me, wagging his tail hopefully.

"Can you get the silverware?" Mom asks. "RJ, turn off the game and come eat."

I get the knives and forks. Mom's already put plates on the table. The kitchen smells of garlic knots, which sort of makes up for not getting sushi. I grab one and bite into the buttery, doughy, garlicky goodness.

"Sammy stole a garlic knot!" RJ tattles. Like I said, he's a human killjoy.

"Can you at least pretend to be civilized and wait till you sit down to eat?" Mom sighs. She pours herself a glass of wine and takes a big slug of it as soon as she slumps into her chair.

"Not really," I say. "I am undone by the smell of garlic knots."

RJ reaches across the table with two grabby hands and takes one knot in each.

"Mom!" I exclaim, pointing at my brother. "You call that civilized?"

"One at a time, RJ!" Mom says. "I don't know where I went wrong . . ." she mutters.

RJ throws one of the garlic knots back onto the plate.

"*Ewww!* Don't put it back after you've touched it with your germy hands!"

"Make up your mind!" RJ complains. "Can I take it or not?"

"Now that you've touched it, take it," Mom says. "But from now on, only take one at a time."

RJ takes back his germ-infested garlic knot, and Mom serves out the lasagna and passes around the salad. She makes us each take some salad, even though neither of us are big lettuce fans. We get that from Dad, who always used to say, "Lettuce is for rabbits," until RJ did a report on rabbits in third grade and learned that's a suburban legend—lettuce can be really bad for a rabbit's digestive system. After that, Dad had to change his tune, although this knowledge didn't make any of us like lettuce any more, nor did it stop Mom from trying to force us to eat it.

"How come Dad's working late again?" RJ asks. "Is it because of the protesters?"

"Yes." Mom sighs.

"Why are they protesting about company profits? It's stupid. Making a profit is what companies are supposed to do, isn't it?" I point out.

"Duh!" RJ comments with his mouth full of half-chewed lasagna.

"Can you not talk with your mouth full?" I tell him.

"Making a profit is, indeed, what companies are supposed to do," Mom says, knocking back the rest of her wine. "But it's not just about profits. According to the great unwashed camp outside the bank, corporations in general, and banks in particular, are engaged in a sinister conspiracy to take over the world. They're also responsible for the financial crisis, the decline of Western civilization, wars, poverty, the latest *Star Wars* movie not living up to their expectations, and so on. In short, Banks Are the Devil."

"Which they aren't," RJ says, thankfully without any food in his mouth this time. "Because that's just crazy."

I have to agree with my brother on that. The thought of Dad being involved in a sinister plot of any kind is just laughable. Sure, he can be strict at times, but Dr. Evil? No way.

"Doesn't Dad have a PR department to deal with this stuff?" I ask. "Why does he have to stay late every night?"

"Because he's the CEO," Mom says. "When you're the head of the company, the buck stops with you. Your dad takes his responsibilities very seriously. He's worried about the security and safety of the company and everyone who works there."

"What do you mean security and safety? Could things get violent?" RJ's wide eyes reflect the overhead light fixture and fear for our dad.

"Everything will be fine," Mom says, realizing her mistake a minute too late. She reaches across the table to pat RJ's hand comfortingly, but he pulls it away.

My brother is one of those kids who wakes up in the middle of the night screaming because he's had some crazy dream about an asteroid colliding with Earth and everything being destroyed, or a plane crashing into our house and killing everyone or a coyote eating Scruffles. You can tell him it was just a dream, but from the way his hair is stuck to his head in a cold dripping sweat, you know to him it was as good as real. When he had the coyote-eating-Scruffles dream, Dad had to let the dog sleep in RJ's bed for the rest of the night, even though at the time he wasn't allowed. That was the end of the No Dogs on the Bed rule.

I'll be falling asleep with my earbuds in tonight so RJ doesn't wake me up if he starts freaking out at some ungodly hour. I can feel a huge zit erupting on my chin, and that means I need my beauty rest even more than usual.

Mom runs her finger around the rim of the empty wineglass. "Your dad thinks the protesters will get tired of camping out in front of headquarters and leave soon," she says. "And if they don't leave on their own, the city will encourage them to vacate because they're impacting so many other businesses nearby."

"Encourage them?" I ask. "Or force them?"

"Will there be riots?" RJ is really starting to freak now.

Mom gives me an irritated glance. Of course it's my fault for asking a simple question, not RJ's for being hypersensitive about everything.

"I'm sure when and if the time comes, the city will handle things in such a way that the site is cleared without incident," Mom says, sounding every inch like the consultant she's paid to be.

RJ looks only half-convinced. "As long as Dad's okay," he says.

I try to imagine what would inspire me to camp out in front of Dad's building—or, for that matter, anywhere in New York City. It's not exactly my idea of a good time. I don't even like camping when it's in a beautiful forest. There are too many bugs and no bathrooms or cell service. But camping where the street is dirty and smells like pee is even less my thing. Going to concerts and the theater and shopping in cool vintage stores—that's more my jam.

"He'll be fine," Mom assures RJ. "It's just a stressful time."

She fills her wineglass all the way to the top. Looks like it's a stressful time for Mom, too.

After dinner, when I'm up in my room, I take a cute picture of Scruffles, with his big brown puppy eyes.

scruffles misses you, I text to Dad. **so do i.**

Awww. Miss you both, Dad texts back. Hope I get back before you go to bed. Love, Dad.

My dad definitely texts like an old person.

you don't have to write "Love, Dad." i know it's you! :P

I take a screenshot and send him a picture of our convo.

see, it says "dad" at the top of the screen! : D

Parents are so quaint.

Putting down my phone, I open my laptop to make a start on my homework. Scruffles jumps on the bed and rests his head on my foot.

"Let's hope this stupid protest ends soon," I murmur to him, and the end of his tail flutters in agreement.

There's enough stress in my life right now.

March 28

I'm not sure how I can stand to live in the same house as my mom for another year and a half without either (a) committing matricide, or (b) my head exploding.

Nothing I do is right. I can't wait to go to college. Too bad I have to jump over so many insane hurdles in the next few months in order to get there. NO PRESSURE, RIGHT?!

Speaking of pressure, it's 58 days till prom (but who's counting?) and I still don't have a date. The good news is that as far as I can tell, Jamie Moss still doesn't have a date, either, which means there's a chance he's going to ask me.

If Dad wasn't stuck at work 24/7, he would be logical and tell me to start making decision trees like I've been learning about in AP Statistics. Like where you consider the probability of each outcome and assign a weighted preference to each one so you can make a rational decision. (Geeky much?) That's assuming this whole dating thing is rational in the first place, a point about which I am not entirely convinced.

But working on the assumption that it is, let's say there's only a 15% probability that Jamie would ask me first, and an 85% probability that AN Other would, I'd then assign my preferences for the various outcomes to see what I should do.

Okay, I actually just tried doing that. Apparently I'm still very much my father's daughter, even when he isn't here.

The problem is trying to figure out the actual probability of Jamie asking me. How do you know when a guy really likes you? How do you figure out if your probability estimate is legit or wishful thinking?

You'd have thought they'd have an app for that by now, but they don't. What's the matter with you, Apple? You should be all over this!

Just imagine how much easier life would be if you could download an app and enter—or better yet, record, except I think that might be illegal (note to self: check)—your interactions with a guy, and then use a database of male speech info to estimate the probability he will actually ask you out. It's pure genius—and it would eliminate so much heartbreak. Why hasn't anyone done it yet?

My talents are wasted at Brooklawne High.

Given lack of said technology, I have to base my predictions on the scientific observations below:

1. Subject talks to me before class in an animated way. +

2. This often involves conversations about homework problems that Subject hasn't done yet, but knows I have. −

3. But not always. +

4. Subject laughs at most of my jokes. +

5. 8 out of 10 times, Subject acknowledges me in the hall and smiles and says hi. The other 20% of times, I'm pretty sure it's because he didn't see me. +

6. Subject also seen talking to Geneva Grady in animated way. −

7. Geneva Grady is an airhead who almost got laughed out of social studies in fifth grade because she thought the South won the Civil War, which according to her took place in 1965. I mean, seriously. +

8. But GG is really pretty. −

9. Like probably is going to be nominated for Prom Queen pretty. −

10. But Subject asks me for my homework, not GG, so he clearly thinks I have superior brain power, which has to count for something, right? +

Also, Jamie told GG to get lost today so he could talk to me—even if it was so he could ask me for my homework. And he told me I should come to the next home game. I still don't get why my school spirit depends on attending an athletic event, but if it will improve my prom probability, then maybe it's worth sacrificing a Lighthouse Book Club meeting.

So based on the above data, the original decision tree looked like this:

Prom Decision Tree

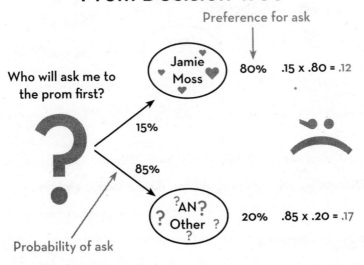

Preference for ask

Who will ask me to the prom first?

Jamie Moss

80%   .15 x .80 = .12

15%

85%

?AN? Other ?

20%   .85 x .20 = .17

Probability of ask

But here's where I'm definitely NOT Dad's daughter: Since the weight of my preferred options isn't going to change, I kept changing the probability percentages till it gave me the answer I wanted, which is wait till Jamie asks me, even though I'm not totally sure if that has a 25% probability.

Prom Decision Tree*

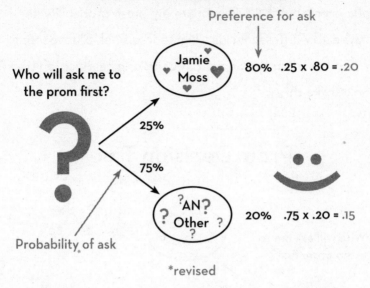

Preference for ask

Who will ask me to the prom first?

Jamie Moss ♥♥♥♥♥♥

80%   .25 x .80 = .20

25%

75%

?AN? Other ?

20%   .75 x .20 = .15

Probability of ask

*revised

I'm never going to Las Vegas or Atlantic City, because there is a very high probability I'd be a lousy gambler.

Mom and Dad went to Vegas last year. Dad had some business meeting there and Mom went with him as a "corporate spouse." They took a picture in front of the fake Eiffel Tower, and Mom framed it next to a picture of them in front of the real Eiffel Tower. My parents thought this was the funniest thing EVER. It must be sad to be old and have so few amusements.

Speaking of which, I wonder if Mom's hitting the wine so hard at dinner because it's finally occurred to her that she and Dad are on the downward slope of life and it won't be long till they're sitting around complaining about how all their friends are wearing Depends and dying. I mean, sure, my life is a bit of a grind at the moment with the SAT and APs and driving lessons. But all that work is leading to something. To a future. To getting out of this house and not always being told what I can and can't do by the Dual Dictators. Otherwise, why be such a good little hamster girl, running endless circles on my academic wheel?

TWO

Rosa, Margo, and I are sitting in the cafeteria the next day at lunch discussing what to wear to the Einstein's Encounter concert, when we're interrupted by a loud obnoxious clown horn.

Gary Harvey, the resident class clown since he moved here in sixth grade, is riding around on a unicycle, carrying what looks like fifty balloons in one hand and the horn, which he is squeezing nonstop, in the other. I'm surprised the balloons haven't carried him away like that old guy in *UP*.

He laps the cafeteria, just to make sure he has everyone's attention, which of course he does, because that horn is so annoying it's impossible to ignore. Then he cycles over to BethAnn Jackson, who looks like she wants to crawl under the table from embarrassment, and hands her the balloons. She takes them reluctantly, like he's just handed her a bouquet of frozen dog-poopsicles. Then Gary drops the horn, reaches into his backpack, and takes out four balls, which he starts juggling.

"Yo, BethAnn,

Girl, you so fine.

Be my date for prom.

Have a ballin' time.

So tell me, girl,

Wanna hear you say

'Affirm-a-tory'

Is comin' my way."

Rapping is definitely not Gary's superpower.

He finishes by throwing the balls across the cafeteria, where one lands in someone's mac and cheese, and another knocks over a carton of milk. The third hits Mr. Severo from the facilities staff in the head, and the last sinks perfectly in a garbage can, earning applause and cheers from everyone sitting nearby.

BethAnn's looking down at the floor as if willing it to swallow her whole. Her arms hug her waist protectively.

Gary's got two friends of his taking footage with their cells for the inevitable YouTube video. Phil Dobens is up in BethAnn's face to get her reaction. Valerie Chen waves him away.

People start chanting "AFFIRM-A-TORY! AFFIRM-A-TORY!" and Gary stands there looking pleased with himself.

He's got the crowd on his side. BethAnn will come off like a jerk if she says no, even though it's pretty clear she doesn't want to go with him.

BethAnn looks like an animal cornered by hunters. While this is going on, I glance over at Jamie Moss, who is sitting three tables away. Of course I know where he's sitting because in our cafeteria there's a seating hierarchy so rigid it's almost assigned seating, and even if there weren't, I'd always be conscious of where he is, because his presence is one of which I am always conscious. I imagine that our eyes will meet across the crowded, noisy cafeteria, and everything will become quiet—his lips will part as he smiles, revealing those white, perfect teeth, and we will have a moment, and he will nod, meaningfully, telling me that my promposal is coming.

Except that he's so busy laughing at BethAnn's awkward situation with his lacrosse teammates that he isn't looking in my direction. At all.

I think about last night's decision trees. Maybe I need to adjust my probabilities to make them a little more realistic. It is a universally acknowledged truth that if a guy doesn't even look at you, there isn't a high probability he'll ask you to prom.

But on the other hand, maybe Jamie's like Mr. Darcy in *Pride and Prejudice*. Maybe he sends smoldering glances in my direction when I'm not looking because he's too proud to do it when I am.

I decide to leave the probabilities where they are.

BethAnn has apparently whispered a quiet, mortified "Affirm-a-tory," and the entire cafeteria starts whooping and hollering. The entire cafeteria except BethAnn and her friends and me. As I watch Gary get on his unicycle and do a victory lap around the cafeteria, pumping his fists in the air and crowing, "All right!" and "Who's the man?!" with Jeremiah and Phil continuing to document every move, including the impending arrival of Mr. Walsh, the assistant principal, who has apparently been informed about the assault of one of the janitorial staff with a juggling ball, I can't help thinking this has been more about him than about BethAnn.

"Well, that was fun," Margo says.

"For *us*, maybe," I say.

"Yeah, it was pretty awkward," Rosa agrees. "You couldn't pay me to be BethAnn Jackson right about now."

"Do you think she'll tell him no later?" I wonder.

"That's not fair," Margo says. "After she said yes in front of the entire cafeteria."

"But what else could she say?" I argue. "He made it impossible for her to say no without looking ungrateful and . . . I don't know . . . mean. Like she was trying to publicly humiliate him, when really she just didn't want to go to prom with him."

"So what—are you saying you wouldn't want a promposal?" Margo asks, her eyebrow raised skeptically.

She's got me there. I've spent far too many hours dreaming of the elaborate and adorable ways that Jamie Moss will ask me to prom.

"No . . . I guess the difference is if you want to go with the guy who asks you," I reply.

"But how is he supposed to know until he asks you?" Rosa says.

"Exactly," Margo says. "So if you want a promposal, you can't blame the guy for trying, right?"

"I guess not," I admit.

Still, as I watch BethAnn rush out of the cafeteria with a friend on either side acting like bodyguards, I wonder, deep down, if I can.

"So what are you wearing to the concert?" Margo asks me.

"I haven't decided yet," I say. "My mom has this sweater that I'm thinking of borrowing."

Of course, I can't ask to borrow it for a concert I'm not supposed to be going to in the first place. But my mom has so many clothes, she won't notice it's missing for one night.

"Seriously?" Margo looks dumbfounded. "There's not a single thing in my mom's closet I'd be caught dead wearing. She is the height of unfashionable."

"I borrow stuff from my mom," Rosa says. "I just have to make sure I ask or else she goes ballistic."

Mom can't find out I borrowed her sweater, because trust me, if she does, she'll go ballistic, too.

My dad makes it home for dinner for the first time all week. He looks tired but smiles when I walk into the kitchen.

"I've missed seeing my Sammy," he says, getting up from the table and enfolding me in a big Dad hug.

His familiar citrusy aftershave mingles with the smell of coffee and sweat.

"I missed you, too," I mumble into his shoulder.

He releases me and holds me at arm's length, his hands on my shoulders. "I think you've grown another inch in the last week," he says.

I shrug, so his hands fall off my shoulders. "It's just your imagination," I say. "I'm still the same."

Dad sits back down, the smile erased from his face.

"Maybe it is just my imagination," he says. "Because when I have weeks like this, when I leave for work before you get up and get back after you're asleep, it feels like you're growing up without me."

He sounds angry, and I wonder if he's mad at me, which would be totally unfair because it's not like I can help growing up.

"Well, you're home tonight," I say. "Does that mean you got rid of the protesters?"

Dad gives a grim chuckle. "I wish I could just *get rid* of them. But we live in a democracy, and apparently they're entitled to their First Amendment right of free speech, even if it's disrupting the livelihoods of all the businesses in the vicinity."

"I thought the mayor was going to—" my mom starts to say.

"Let's not talk about that tonight," Dad says to cut Mom off. "Not when I'm finally home with the kids."

My phone buzzes with a text. I look down and see it's from Rosa in the concert group chat, but Dad's talking to me.

"So how's it going with the driving?"

"Great," I say.

"Are you ready for the test?" Dad asks.

"Definitely."

"I'm not so sure," Mom says.

No. Way.

"Are you serious, Mom?" I explode. "I'm a really good driver!"

"What about your AP exams?" Dad interjects, trying to head off World War III. "Do you feel prepared?"

Dad doesn't want to talk about work when he comes home after a long week. Doesn't he get that the last thing I feel like talking about are all the Very Important Tests I have to take in the next few weeks?

"Well, I'm not prepared *yet*," I tell him. "I've still got a month to study."

I'm saved from further interrogation about my exam readiness by my brother, whose entrance not only takes the heat off me but allows me to read the text from Rosa.

only 8 more days till einstein's encounter! followed by about twenty different emoticons that express excitement and happiness.

i know! i'm excited, too, but not quite as emoticrazy!

Rosa responds with five more lines of emoticons.

"Sammy, no devices at the table," Mom reminds me as she puts the casserole on the table. "You know the rules."

"But we haven't started eating yet!" I protest.

"Just put it away, Samantha," Dad says. "I'm finally home in time for dinner. Let's enjoy it together, without distractions."

Just then, his phone buzzes with a text and he reaches into his pocket to look at it.

"You said without distractions, Dad."

He opens his mouth as if he's about to tell me it's work and important, but RJ says, "Busted!"

Dad grins sheepishly. "I guess I am, aren't I?" he says, ruffling RJ's hair. "C'mon, let's eat. I want to hear about everything I've missed."

I can't talk about the stuff that's really on my mind: how Mom is so annoying, how I'm worried about the probability of Jamie Moss asking me to prom, how bad I feel for BethAnn Jackson because she was pressured into saying yes to going to prom with Gary Harvey because he asked her in front of the entire cafeteria, and how I'm scared because what if that happens to me.

Instead, I just talk to him about the things I want to forget but that he always wants to talk about constantly—all the upcoming tests that matter so much to my future.

April 5

I'm starting to I wonder if my parents are right about something. They've always been so annoying about promposals.
Like, "Back in the Jurassic Age when we were in high school,
a guy just went up to a girl and said, 'Do you want to go to
the prom?' Simple as that. No fuss, no big production, just
a simple yes or no answer. Done." Or "What is it with young
people today that they have to make a public spectacle out
of every single minute of their lives? Some things are
best done with a little intimacy." *Cue sidelong glance at
each other accompanied by vomit-inducing smirk, which
makes me leave the room, because seriously, Helene and
Dick, I really don't want to think about you guys doing that.
EVER.

But cringe-worthy parental innuendo aside, after the
Gary Harvey/BethAnn Jackson promposal fiasco, I think
the Fossils might have a point. Two days after the scene
in the cafeteria—but after Gary edited his footage and
posted it to YouTube and it started making the rounds on
social media as "Awesome Cafeteria Promposal"—BethAnn
called him and told him that she wasn't going to go with
him after all. Depending on who you listen to, she: "felt

pressured into saying yes because he asked her in front of the whole cafeteria and everyone was chanting." That's the story according to BethAnn and her friends. But according to the second video Gary made and posted on YouTube, which is getting much wider distribution (unfortunately for BethAnn), she's an ungrateful skank who went back on her word after all the wonderful things he did for her.

It's a five-minute video that cuts footage of the promposal with close-ups of Gary's irate face in full-on rant. You can actually see spit coming out of his mouth a few times. It's gross.

But like I said, his version of events is the one that's spreading far and wide, especially after the website TechBrotainment front-paged both the videos the day before yesterday. As of ten minutes ago, Gary's rant has over 538,439 views and the number is growing hourly.

BethAnn didn't come to school today. After reading the comments on TechBrotainment, I don't think I'd want to show my face in public ever again.

The people who are judging BethAnn and finding her guilty of all kinds of crimes against Gary weren't there. They only saw the parts that Gary showed them. But that doesn't stop them from being convinced they know the truth about what happened.

I felt bad for BethAnn at the time, but now I feel even worse for her. And mad, too. Prom is supposed to be fun. No one should be obligated to go just because someone asked them. It's supposed to be a choice, isn't it?

As much as I thought I wanted a big adorable promposal from Jamie Moss that the whole world could see, now I think I'd be happy if he just asked me the old-school way. Quietly. Privately. No video. Save the fireworks for the prom.

Who am I kidding? I'll be happy if Jamie asks me, period.

THRee

The afternoon of the Einstein's Encounter concert, I have Dad drop me off at the library in keeping with my AP Gov study-group fiction. He's on the way into the city for some important hush-hush meeting with city officials. I only know about it because I overheard him telling Mom when I was scoping their location so I could go into their room and borrow Mom's sweater. Rosa's mom is picking me up from the library and driving us to Margo's.

"Study hard," Dad says.

"Don't I always?"

He leans over to kiss the side of my face, where the hair meets my temple. "I like that shampoo," he says. "It smells like the vacation I could really use right now."

It's times like this I wonder how my father ever managed to get a date, much less get married, reproduce, and become the CEO of a major financial institution.

"My hair smells like a *vacation*?"

Dad laughs with a rueful smile. "I never was much of a . . . what do you call it these days . . . a *player*?"

"Oh my god, Dad. Don't. *Ever.* Say. That. Again."

"What I *meant* was that your hair smells like coconut, which reminds me of suntan lotion, which reminds me of taking a vacation," Dad explains.

My father's brain is a very strange place.

"That *almost* makes sense, in a bizarre random way. But don't ever say it in public."

"Never mind," he says. "Have fun. I'll see you tomorrow."

I wave good-bye to Dad as he drives away, and I feel a twinge of guilt about the fact that I'm lying to him, but it's gone by the time I reach the library steps. Because in a matter of hours, I'm going to be in the presence of super-hot Davy Linklater, lead singer of Einstein's Encounter.

I definitely need to change first.

i'm at the library, I text Rosa.

kk. we'll be there in about five minutes.

I brought my AP Gov book as cover, but I'm too excited about the concert to actually take it out and study. Since it's sunny, I sit on the front steps of the library, close my eyes, and soak up some rays.

Davy Linklater is smiling at me from the stage and we are having a serious moment when "Hey, Sammy, are you here for the gov study group?" yanks me from my daydream.

Kate Pierce is standing over me, blocking out the sun.

There's a gov study group tonight? For reals? I thought I made that up.

Then I remember some post in the AP Gov Facebook group, which I must have seen enough to give me the idea to use Kate's name but then forgotten about.

"Oh . . . I . . . actually, I came earlier to study," I tell her. "I've got plans tonight."

"Too bad," she says. "Well, next time."

"Definitely," I tell her as she heads inside.

I'm thumbing through my phone when a voice says, "You look way too bored for such a sunny day."

I glance up and see Noah Woods. He's wearing a T-shirt with a picture of Winston Churchill with one of his quotes: "Attitude is a little thing that makes a big difference."

The afternoon sun glints off his dark curls like a reddish-gold halo, bringing out the amber at the center of his hazel eyes. Noah has really nice eyes, I've noticed.

"Oh, hey, Noah. Love your T-shirt."

"Cool, isn't it? I got it in SoHo."

"My dad would go crazy for it. He's a Churchill freak."

"So's my grandpa," Noah says. "He's coming over and bringing the DVD of the movie *Gallipoli* this weekend. Watching historically themed movies is this thing we do."

"That's . . . unusual," I say.

He's wary, suddenly. "Unusual as in . . . ?"

"That came out wrong," I say, my face flushing. "I mean, unusual as in that it's really cool that you and your grandpa share something like that."

"Oh," he says, clearly relieved. He sits down next to me. "So, are you here to check out the new book club book or to study?"

I hesitate, trying to figure out which lie to tell him, but then I see Mrs. Jiménez's car turning into the parking lot, so I decide to tell him the truth.

"Actually, I'm heading into the city for a concert," I admit. "Einstein's Encounter at the Bowery Ballroom."

"Seriously? I love Einstein's Encounter." He sings the opening lines of "Whispering Courage," my absolute favorite song.

Turns out, Noah has a decent singing voice, and hearing him sing the words that mean so much to me is pretty hot. Who knew?

"Rosa's here to get me," I tell him reluctantly as Mrs. Jiménez pulls up to the curb. Rosa rolls down the window and gestures for me to hurry up.

"Have fun," Noah says with a lazy grin. "I expect a full report and set list on Monday."

I grin back at him.

Margo's room looks like a beach town in the aftermath of a Category 5 hurricane when Rosa and I get there. The only reason there are any clothes left in her closet is because she has so many.

"I don't have anything to wear!" she wails.

Rosa gives me the *She's loco* look.

"I'm pretty sure you do," I tell Margo. "The problem is finding anything in this . . . this . . ."

"Disaster area?" Rosa fills in the blank.

"It's a mess because I can't find anything to wear," Margo complains. "What do you think about this?"

She holds up a black minidress and a pair of matching tights.

"Perfect," Rosa and I say in unison, anxious to start getting dressed ourselves.

Rosa's wearing jeans and a lace shirt with a tank top underneath and, as always, heels because she is so worried about being short. I'm not exactly tall, but I'm grateful for the few extra inches that let me get away with wearing lower heels. I hate having sore feet.

"*Love* that sweater!" Rosa exclaims as I pull Mom's sweater out of my bag.

"It's my mom's," I admit. "She doesn't know I borrowed it. If anything happens to it, I'm dead." I pull out the rest of my outfit, tight black jeans and my vintage motorcycle ankle boots.

Margo stops dressing and stares at me. "You took your Mom's sweater without asking?" she says. She reaches over and looks at the label. "That thing's designer."

I take off the T-shirt I'm wearing and slip the sweater over my head. "Nothing's going to happen. It'll be fine," I say.

"It does look hot on you, *chica*," Rosa says, checking me out. I smile, and then she shoves me onto the bed and starts attacking my hair. By the time she's done, it's in the perfect messy bun, piled on top of my head with only a few wild curls escaping.

"There. Now you're ready," she announces, satisfied.

"Hard to argue with the finished look," Margo says with approval, pulling on her hot-pink high-top Chucks. "Let's go!"

Mrs. McHenry drives us to the station to catch the 6:35 p.m. train.

"Be careful, watch your wallets, and don't take a drink from an open bottle," she warns as we're getting out of the car.

"*Mooooom!*" Margo groans. "How many times have I been to the city before?"

"It never hurts to be reminded," Mrs. McHenry says. "Call to let me know what train you're on coming home."

We all wave as the car pulls away.

"My mom is such a freak," Margo says.

"Not especially," I assure her. "Helene is waaaaaaay worse."

"Trust me, she's not," Margo says. "I can't wait to go to college so I can escape from her freakiness."

Agreed. It's just everything in between that is such an ordeal.

"Can we make tonight a college-free zone?" I suggest. "It's all anyone ever talks about. Especially parents."

"I know!" Rosa agrees. *"Where are you looking? What are your safeties?"* She's putting on different parent imitation voices for each question. *"Have you visited anywhere yet? What's your top pick?"*

"What are you planning to study?" Margo continues. *"Oh, so you want to be unemployed when you graduate?"*

By the time we get on the train, we've sworn a pact that college and APs and Future Life Plans are strictly forbidden subjects.

Prom, however, is not.

"Madison Maguire said that Dan Bates is going to ask me next week," Margo tells us. "I wish he'd hurry it up. I don't want everyone else to get the best dresses first."

There's a junior girls secret Instagram feed where you post the dress you bought so no one buys the same one. In theory, anyway. Last year, three girls showed up in the same dress, and according to people who were there, security had to get involved.

I'm less worried about getting the right dress than I am the right date.

"I think Eddy Lau is going to ask me," Rosa says. "He was hinting in physics. You know, asking if I had a date yet and stuff."

"Do you want to go with him?" Margo asks.

"Sure," Rosa says. "He's funny. And cute."

"Quiet, though."

"Only till you get to know him," Rosa says. "Which I have, because we've been lab partners this year. What about you?"

"Well . . ." I hesitate, afraid to tell even my best friends about my deepest wish. "I'm hoping that Jamie Moss will ask me."

The silence after my revelation is deafening.

"Really?" Rosa sounds surprised. I mean, I know I haven't exactly been going around talking about how gorgeous I think he is, but that's only because I didn't feel the need to state the obvious.

"Yes, really."

She shrugs. "Cool. I hope he asks you."

Margo is staring out the window. Her lack of comment is like a comment itself.

"What, Margo?"

"Nothing."

"Come on, tell me!"

She hesitates. "He just . . . doesn't seem like your type."

"What is *my type* exactly?"

"I don't know. Smarter. Funnier. Not as . . . I don't know. Just not Jamie."

The way Noah looked as he sang "Whispering Courage" pops into my mind. I shake my head. He's not the one who is supposed to be there.

It feels like there's something she's not telling me, but I don't want to push it. Because we're going to a concert and being in the city without my parents' permission means excitement and possibility, especially tonight, when we're on our way to see one of my favorite bands in the entire world.

When we get to Grand Central, I can almost feel my blood fizzing in my veins. We take the subway downtown, and when we get out, we look in store windows, admire street fashion, and take pictures of the guy with the sandwich boards telling us that the world is coming to an end in the next thirty days unless we all repent and accept Jesus as our Personal Savior.

"I guess if the asteroid hits before prom, it'll be all my fault," I joke.

"Not mine," Margo says. "I've been learning catechism since I was six."

We walk down the street, singing "It's the End of the World as We Know It," confident that even if the world might be coming to an end, our night is just beginning.

There's already a crowd outside the Bowery Ballroom.

We wait in line, have our purses searched, and are asked to show ID. After seeing the birth dates on our driver's permits, a bouncer attaches white wristbands, with "Under 21" in big red letters, to our wrists, making sure they're tight enough that we can't slide them off to exchange them with someone who is drinking age.

"I feel like Hester Prynne," Rosa grumbles.

"Yeah, could they make our scarlet letters any bigger?" Margo says. "They could at least make them a cool color instead of making it look like we'll need to be carted away in an ambulance."

"They probably make them this obvious so we *don't* end up being carted away in an ambulance," I point out.

Margo gives me a dirty look. "Stop, Sammy. You sound like a mom."

Hearing the word *mom* makes me nervous. I don't want to think about moms while I'm wearing mine's clothing at a concert I snuck out to.

The warm-up band, Oversized Aviators, has already started by the time we enter, but the place still isn't even half full. Rosa, being cute and petite, is surprisingly good at weaving her way through crowds, so we follow her lead and manage to get within ten feet of the stage.

It's crowded up this close, even for the opening act. I'm wedged between Rosa and an older hipster couple. Behind us is a group of guys from NYU who are either seniors or who have fake IDs, because they're all holding drinks of an alcoholic nature.

"Do you think we can ask those guys to buy us a beer?" Margo says to Rosa and me between songs.

"Are you crazy?" Rosa hisses. "I'm not taking a drink from some strange guy."

"But we could go to the bar with him and watch the whole time," Margo argues.

"Yeah, and then the bartender will see our wristbands," I point out. "Besides, I feel guilty enough being here when I'm not supposed to *and* wearing my mother's illegally borrowed sweater. I don't need to add underage drinking to my list of transgressions."

"But maybe next time!" Rosa says brightly.

I laugh.

"You guys need to learn how to live a little." Margo sighs.

"Us guys need to get into a good college," I say.

"College?" one of the guys behind us shouts over the song that's just starting. "What college do you go to?"

Rosa, Margo, and I glance at one another, and I can tell we're all thinking the same thing.

"Barnard," Rosa says.

"Ooh, *smart girls*," he says to his buddies. "Watch out, guys. These girls are smart *and* cute."

We're also not drunk, which means that we're much better at standing upright than he is.

"How is this guy going to make it through the whole concert if he's already this wasted?" I ask Rosa and Margo.

"Good question," Margo says.

"Are you into Oversized Aviators?" one of Drunk Guy's friends asks us.

"They're okay," I say. "But we're really here for Einstein's Encounter."

"Yeah, they're legendary," he says. "Hey, do any of you girls want a drink?"

"Thanks, I'm good," I tell him, giving Margo a warning glance in case she's getting any ideas.

"Yeah, us too," Rosa says, not even giving Margo a chance to open her mouth.

"Okay, later," he says, heading for the bar, followed by Other Drunk Guy, who weaves behind him like a human metronome.

The place is getting more and more crowded as Oversized Aviators finish and we wait for Einstein's Encounter to start. The hipster couple on my right is talking loudly about politics, and I overhear them mention the protest at Dad's bank.

"NPR reported that Wallach and the mayor are bringing in the riot squad to clear the protest," Hipster Guy says. "Fascists."

My dad is one of those fascists.

"But what about the protesters' rights?" Hipster Girl asks.

"The judge ruled that the First Amendment gives them a right to speech, but not to camp out," Hipster Guy says. "Realistically, how long are they going to be able to stay there without tents?"

"Not long—especially if it rains." Hipster Girl sighs. "Why does The Man always win?"

"Is that your dad's company they're talking about?" Margo asks.

"Quiet!" I hiss. "I don't want them to know Dick and I are related. They side with the protesters."

"So is your dad 'The Man'?" Rosa snorts.

"I always thought he was just 'The Dad,' but apparently he's also 'The Man,'" I tell her.

I'd totally tease Dad about that, except I can't tell him where I heard it. In theory, I'm not here.

The drunk guys return just as the lights dim, and Einstein's Encounter takes the stage, opening with "Humor in an Elevator." I'm in heaven. Davy Linklater is wearing black jeans and a T-shirt that says "Why?" which is so . . . *profound*. Not only is he gorgeous with an amazing voice, he clearly asks the big questions.

"This is epic!" Rosa shouts.

"I know!" I yell back.

Margo screams, "I love you guys!"

At one point, Davy actually smiles at us—or at least in our direction. Truthfully, I can't tell if it's for us or the drunk NYU guys, who have been getting progressively drunker during the show. The drunkest one keeps shouting out requests for songs by other bands. It's beyond annoying.

But then I hear the opening chords to "Whispering

Courage," and I can't help but be swept up in the moment and the music. I can feel the bass in my chest and I inhale the guitar chords with each breath. My hips move in perfect synchronicity to the beat of the drums, and I sing the chorus along with the other five hundred people here: "You don't have to shout, or shoot, because your whispering courage will conquer them all."

It's the perfect moment.

Suddenly, something warm and slimy lands on the back of my neck. Rosa screams. Then the smell hits me.

"Oh my god. HE THREW UP ON ME!" Rosa is hysterical. "It's all over my back!"

"You idiot!" Margo shouts at Drunk Guy, who is bending over, staring at the puddle of vomit on the floor with a stupid, dazed expression. "You got me, too!"

"He's sorry," Drunk Guy's friend says. "Really sorry."

"No, he's not," I snap. "He's too drunk to even know he's sorry."

"I'm covered in puke!" Rosa wails, like this isn't obvious to anyone with a nose.

"Let's go," I say, with one longing glance back at the stage.

We make our way through the crowd to the lobby, which isn't at all hard despite the fact that everyone is dancing like crazy to a fantastic version of "Typing Liberals." When you're with someone covered in vomit, even the most packed crowd parts like the Red Sea.

I spot the merch booth and head that way.

"Look, you can get a band tee to change into," I tell Rosa. "I might get one, too, because El Drunko got my back with spatter."

"Me too," Margo said. "It's making me gag just to smell myself."

Perfect plan, till we find out the cheapest T-shirt is twenty dollars. I can't use my debit card. My parents see the activity on the card and it would be a giveaway that I wasn't where I said I would be. The problem is, after paying for a bottle of water, my round-trip train ticket, and a MetroCard, I only have thirteen dollars left.

"Can either of you lend me seven dollars?" I ask.

"I don't have enough, either," Margo says.

"Can't you use a card?" I ask.

Margo holds up her tiny cell phone case/purse on a strap. "I didn't bring one. All I brought was money, ID, and my phone."

Both of us look at Rosa.

"Don't look at me. My mom told me not to bring a card in case I got pickpocketed. I have enough for one T-shirt. And I'm the one who needs it the most."

We can't argue with that. The back of her shirt suffered the direct hit, and Margo's and mine only suffered collateral damage, however disgusting-smelling it might be. We're just going to have to try to wash off the best we can and suffer.

Rosa buys a T-shirt from the girl at the merch booth, who somehow manages the incredible feat of scrunching up her nose in disgust while simultaneously looking down it at us. I'll have to practice that trick in the mirror sometime—when I don't reek of vomit.

We go to the bathroom and attempt to repair the damage. From inside the concert hall, we can hear the crowd going wild.

"I can't believe we're missing the best part of the show because of that . . . that . . ." Margo can't even come up with an adjective bad enough.

I can.

I pull a bunch of paper towels from the dispenser. "Can you get my back?" I ask Margo. "I'll do yours."

We take turns washing each other's backs, which leaves us with wet shirts, still smelling faintly gross and extremely uncomfortable to wear. But it's better than nothing.

The magic is over. The spell is broken. I just want to go home.

April 7

OMG! IT'S SO EARLY. WHY AM I EVEN AWAKE? I AM
SO TIRED.

Maybe it's because Margo's snoring—she has been
snoring ALL. NIGHT. LONG. If it weren't for the fact that I
would end up in prison for murder, I'd stick a pillow over
her face just to stop that hideous sawing. It's like nails on a
chalkboard to the third power. And the worst part? She
stops just long enough for me to almost drop off again, and
then . . . IT STARTS ALL OVER. Maybe I should take a
recording and then do the pillow thing. No jury of my peers
would convict me if they heard that racket. Seriously, Margo
sounds like a ninety-year-old man.

That's why I've given up trying to sleep. Between that
and Rosa on the other side of me still reeking of puke, it's
no wonder I can't sleep.

Couldn't the girl have taken a shower when we got
back? I was tired and miserable, too, but I still got under
a stream of water and washed every olfactory-offending
odor away. Rosa? She just crashed into bed and went
straight to sleep, despite clearly bearing some of that drunk
NYU guy's upchuck somewhere on her. You'd think she'd

worry more about germs and stuff. Maybe it's a cultural thing.

So here I am, lonely and awake in the cold light of morning, writing about my crushed dreams. God, even I think I'm being lame.

Maybe when you look forward to something too much, it's the Kiss of Death. From now on, I'm cultivating a "Meh" attitude, even when it's something I'm really excited about. Otherwise I'll jinx it and end up miserable, wet, stinking of puke, and terrified of my mom's wrath. So not worth it.

It's not that the Einstein's Encounter concert was a total loss. I got to hear "Humor in an Elevator" and "The Catalyst of My Dreams" and I had one of the most spiritual moments of my life during "Whispering Courage"—at least until the vomitsplosion.

Sometimes I hate other people and think I'd be happiest if I could just stay the rest of my life alone in a cave on a distant mountaintop—as long as I had Wi-Fi and food and running water and a comfortable bed. Okay, maybe not a mountaintop. Maybe I just need to be in my own room away from everyone for a while. Even my best friends, who drove me crazy last night.

Why am I any more of an idiot for liking Jamie Moss than Rosa is for liking Eddy Lau, or Margo is for wanting to go to prom with Danny Bates? They are so judgmental sometimes. Not to mention two-faced. Rosa told me she thinks Danny Bates is a few sandwiches short of a picnic, but she didn't say anything about that when Margo said she thought he was going to ask her to prom. And Margo has laughed about what a Class A nerd Eddy Lau is, but did she say a word about that when Rosa said she was thinking about going to prom with him? Not on your life! But the minute I mention Jamie Moss, the two of them act all weird. What's up with that? Telling me he's not my type . . . I don't even know what my type is, so what makes Margo such an expert?

Whatever. My biggest problem now, besides exhaustion, is dealing with Mom's sweater. In between being mad about the snoring and the puke smell, I've spent half the night worrying about that. Okay, I just looked up ways to clean vomitous luxury garments. Dry cleaning seems to be the only option, but there's no way to do that without Mom finding out.

If only I had my license! But I don't. : ////

I'll figure it out.

FOUR

As soon as it's a civilized hour, I call home to see what's going on so I can figure out where Rosa's mom should drop me in order to maintain the "AP study-group sleepover" fiction.

Mom is in a foul mood.

"Dad had to go into work again," she fumes. "He was supposed to take RJ to his Odyssey of the Mind competition so I could go to the grand opening of Lickety Splits. You're going to have to get a ride home from someone."

"No problem," I say. "Tell RJ good luck!"

"I will. I'm sorry to leave you to your own devices like this, but I've got to go right now if RJ's going to make it on time."

"It's fine, Mom. I can get a ride home."

"Make sure you let Scruffles out," Mom says. "I'm not sure how long this Odyssey thing will run."

"Hopefully not ten years," I quip, referring to how long it took Odysseus to get back to Ithaca after the fall of Troy.

"Don't even joke," Mom groans. "It's bad enough I have to miss my client's big day."

When I hang up, I tell Rosa and Margo about Mom's bad luck and my good fortune.

"Did your dad have to go into the office because they're clearing out the protesters' camp?" Rosa asks.

I hadn't even thought about the protesters and the judge's decision and what those hipsters said at the concert last night. I've been too busy worrying about how to clean up my mom's sweater and get it back into her closet without her noticing it's missing.

"Maybe. I don't know."

"That could get ugly," Margo says. "Do you think they'll bring in the riot squad?"

"Why would they do that?" I say. "It's not like there's going to be a big fight or anything."

"You think?" Margo says. "After they've been camping there for weeks?"

I shrug, because I'm too tired to argue. I just want to take a nap in my own bed in the blissfully odorless quiet of my room.

"Did you girls have a good time last night?" Mrs. Jiménez asks when we get in the car.

Rosa mumbles something incomprehensible in Spanish,

making it clear that covering up last night's disaster is down to me.

"Yeah!" I say with as much enthusiasm as exhaustion and stress about Mom's sweater allows. "It was *unbelievable*."

As in you just wouldn't believe what actually happened, and I'm not going to be the one to tell you. I lean my head against the window and let the rest of the drive pass in silence.

Scruffles greets me with joyous abandon after Mrs. Jiménez drops me off. You'd think I'd been away for a year.

"Hey, cute puppy!" I tell him, scratching behind his ears. "I missed you, too! We're going to play, but first I've got an important job to do."

He looks up at me expectantly, head cocked to one side, as if to say, *Okay, what?*

I head to the washing machine in the basement, with Scruffles following close on my heels, and pull the smelly sweater out of my backpack. I'd done some more research online and found a website that said dry-clean only items can also be washed by hand, but there's a delicate cycle on the washing machine that I figure is pretty much the same thing. I don't want to risk scrubbing any lingering molecules of some random guy's puke off with my actual hands. What happens if he had some deathly communicable disease like Ebola or bird flu or necrotizing fasciitis, that bacterial infection that eats your skin? No, thanks.

Scruffles is sniffing a little too intently at my backpack, and I realize that it smells of vomit, too. I throw it in the machine with the sweater.

While the cycle is running, I go upstairs to study for AP US History. Scruffles comes with and curls up on the bed next to me, his body warm against my hip. I've made flash cards based on old AP exam questions, and I start going through them, one by one.

Scruffles puts his head on my AP book, which is lying open on the bed. He looks like he's studying, too.

I take a picture of him and send it to Dad.

scruffles is studying hard. think he's going to do better on the APUSH exam than I am.

Usually Dad responds quickly, even if he's busy, but this time he doesn't. He still hasn't texted me back forty minutes later, when I go down to take the sweater out of the washing machine.

To my horror, I see that the zipper on my backpack caught a thread of the sweater and pulled it during the wash. There's a snag in the back. I feel sick to my stomach. I am dead. Or I'm going to be if I can't fix this.

I try pulling the thread back through and stretching the sweater to its proper shape. Hopefully Mom won't notice. But it's still pretty obvious it isn't in the pristine state it was when I took it out of the closet. This is turning out to be a complete disaster. Why did I borrow the sweater in the first place? What was I thinking?

According to my online research, the sweater has to be laid flat to dry. If that's going to happen before Mom gets home, I better do it outside. Thankfully Mother Nature is cooperating.

Scruffles follows me out the back door and immediately takes off after a squirrel, which of course he doesn't catch, but it never stops him from trying.

He trots back, tongue hanging from the side of his mouth. It looks like he's smiling. Scruffles has definitely not inherited the Wallach overachiever gene. He doesn't sit around worrying that Mom and Dad are going to freak out and think he's a total failure at life because he didn't catch a squirrel. He just finds the nearest patch of sunshine, flops down, curls up, and takes a nap.

Maybe I should learn from my dog.

But with four AP exams and the SAT coming up, I can't afford to snooze, even though I'm tired from not sleeping well last night. Since it's nice out, I decide to study on the patio, stretching out on one of the chaises with my flash cards.

"What do you think about Manifest Destiny?" I ask Scruffles. "Wasn't it just imperialism by another name?"

Scruffles raises an eyebrow and ignores me. I don't blame

him. It's too nice to study. I close my eyes and think about summer, when maybe I'll be at the beach with Jamie Moss, because we'll be dating after he asks me to prom . . .

High-pitched barking wakes me up. Scruffles is scratching at the back door, and then I hear the garage door opening.

MOM. IS. HOME.

Heart pounding, I grab the sweater, which, thankfully, is almost dry, fling the back door open, and race upstairs, barely able to breathe by the time I get to the top step just as I hear Mom and RJ talking in the kitchen.

I race down the hall to my parents' room, as quietly as I can, and try to fold the sweater as neatly as Mom's other ones. It looks a little lumpy. Whatever. No time to redo it.

I slip the sweater to the bottom of a pile and tiptoe back out to the hall, listening carefully for sounds of RJ. He's not in his room, so I duck into the bathroom and flush, like that's where I've been the whole time. After splashing water on my overheated face, I casually head downstairs as if I've been studying all day and have absolutely nothing to hide. Just call me Bond. Samantha Bond.

RJ is already slumped on the couch in the family room with the TV on.

"How was Odyssey of the Mind?" I ask my mom.

"Awful. RJ's team lost, and there's been a major catastrophe at work that has Dad tearing his hair out," Mom says.

"What happened?"

"After the judge ruled last night, the mayor moved in the riot police early this morning to clear the protesters," Mom explains. "Some of the protesters got hurt because they refused to respect the eviction order. Apparently these people don't believe in obeying the law." She slams her purse down on the counter.

"How badly hurt?" I ask, thinking about the hipster couple at the concert last night.

"Badly enough to end up in the hospital," Mom says. "It's all over the news. But that's not the worst of it."

"What's worse than people being hurt?" I ask, with a rising sense of panic. "Is Dad okay?"

"Physically, yes. But the bank suffered a cyber breach," Mom says, taking some hamburger meat out of the freezer. "The criminals say they've got over fifty terabytes of data and they're going to publish the first cache of documents tomorrow."

"What's a terabyte? Is that a lot?"

"The prefix *tera* comes from the Greek word for monster," Mom says. "So let's put it this way: Fifty terabytes is the Mother of All Monster Hacks."

I refrain from rolling my eyes at my mom's ridiculous explanation. She could have just said yes. Instead, I say, "No wonder Dad's tearing his hair out. What are the documents about?"

"That's what the IT team and the cyber-security consultants are trying to figure out," Mom says, banging the microwave door closed on the frozen meat and pushing the defrost button. "How the hackers got in, what they were able to get, and how bad it's going to be for the company. If they really have fifty terabytes of data, bad is an understatement."

I've always taken my parents at their word that the protesters were crazy, ignorant people who are unemployed and looking for a handout from the real "job creators" of the world like Dad. But if they've managed to hack the supposedly ultra-secure computer systems at the bank, they can't be *that* stupid, can they?

"How bad could it get?" I ask. "Dad's company hasn't done anything wrong, has it? He's not . . . There's no way Dad could end up in jail, right?"

Mom turns and stares at me, shocked. "Samantha Wallach! Why would you say something like that?"

"Nothing! It's just . . ."

"It's just what? Your father is a good man. He wouldn't get involved in illegal activity." She slams the cupboard door. "Which is more than I can say for these cyber punks who are trying to wreak havoc."

"But—"

"Everybody has secrets they don't want the world to

know, Sammy," Mom says. "No matter how upstanding a person they are."

Truth, I think, remembering what I was doing right before I came downstairs.

I feel bad for my dad, but right now I'm more concerned with making sure my own secrets stay hidden.

April 7

I'm worried about Dad. He looked like an old man when he came home. Not as old as Grandpa Marty, but still. I wonder if he's worried about losing his job. If he does, then what will happen to us? Will I still be able to afford to go to college? I have good grades, but not academic-scholarship-to-top-tier-school kind of grades. Just what I need, a little more pressure and anxiety in my life as I go into exampalooza.

How did the hackers get into the bank's computer systems? I mean it's a bank! Isn't it supposed to be extra secure?

Even the bank's computer geeks and their special security consultants don't know yet, according to Dad. They think it might be something called a Darkhotel operation, where they target high-level executives when they log into the hotel Wi-Fi and then trick them into downloading a browser update that's really software that gives them a way of getting a back door into the company's secure networks. Dad said he vaguely remembers downloading some update when he was in a hotel in Germany.

The worst is that they don't even know the full scope of what the hackers have.

Uh-oh. RJ's screaming. He must be having a nightmare . . . Hold, please.

Yep . . . I went into his room just now. He was tangled up in his sheets as if he'd been trying to fight them, and groaning like he was in pain. And then he screamed again.

"RJ, wake up, you're having a bad dream," I said, shaking him gently.

He was totally out of it, like he always is when he comes out of one of his nightmares.

"Whatimizit?" he said.

I told him it was after eleven and asked him what he'd been dreaming about.

"I dreamed that the hackers stole everything. And we woke up and we were sleeping on the ground and it was snowing and we had absolutely nothing. No food. No clothes. No money. They even took Scruffles."

I tried to lighten the mood by joking. "How'd they manage to download the dog?"

"It was a dream, Sammy," RJ said, with an impressive amount of snark for someone who'd just woken up. "If they could download the house, why would the dog be a problem?"

"Good point, little bro," I admitted.

And then he asked me, straight up, if Dad was going to

be okay and if we were going to be okay. You know, us as a family. Like I have any more idea than he does.

But I wanted the poor kid to be able to sleep, so I just flat-out lied to him. I said, "Don't worry, RJ. You know Dad. He's got this under control."

RJ smiled, leaned back against his pillow, and shut his eyes. I guess he's still young enough to believe that's true.

Five

"Any blowback from the concert?" Margo asks me as we walk into school together on Monday.

"So far so good," I tell her. "But it was a close thing with the sweater. I only just got it back in the closet before she got home with RJ."

"Nice!"

"Yeah. Now let's hope she doesn't notice that it seems to have shrunk in the wash, even though I washed it on the delicate cycle."

"That's not good," Margo says. "But if it makes you feel any better, I had to listen to my mother lecturing me all day yesterday about how I shouldn't hang out with Rosa because she's a bad influence."

I stop walking and stare at her. "Rosa? A bad influence? Why would she think that? Rosa's never even had a detention!"

"*I* know that," Margo says. "But she got into the car reeking of puke."

"That wasn't her fault! It was that idiot guy behind us."

"I know!" Margo says, a defensive note starting to creep into her voice. "But my mom . . . Well, she's . . . she didn't believe Rosa was telling the truth."

There's something about how she says her mom didn't believe *Rosa* was telling the truth, and the way she doesn't quite meet my eyes when she says it, that makes me wonder what is going on.

"We all smelled like puke, Margo. You did. I did. We all did," I point out. "We told your mom what happened when we got in the car. So why is Rosa the bad influence? Why not me?"

Margo is still avoiding my gaze, staring down the hall as if the answer to the meaning of life is on one of the posters at the end of it.

"Margo, *why*?" I press her.

She exhales loudly in frustration as she finally turns to look at me.

"Because my mom didn't believe us. After you guys left the next day, I got in major trouble. She thought we'd *all* been drinking and she was going to ground me for a month," Margo says. "*And* she said she was going to call your parents. I couldn't let her do that because then your parents would know you went to the concert."

Just the thought of Mrs. McHenry making that phone call is almost enough to send me into a panicky tailspin. I take a deep breath and remind myself that it didn't happen. That my secret is still safe.

"So you decided to throw Rosa under the bus to save me—and yourself?"

"Because I know my mom would believe it of her," Margo says. "My parents are . . . Well, sometimes they can be . . . you know . . . not very PC or whatever."

I think the word she's looking for is *racist*. And while I hate that Margo let her mom think that about Rosa to save her own skin, at the same time I can't help being grateful that she did it to save mine. And that makes me feel awful.

"It just seems . . . wrong," I say. "*You* were the one who was going to let the drunk college guys buy you a drink. Not Rosa."

"What are you complaining about?" she demands. "I covered for you, Sammy. So you can't tell Rosa about this. Promise me you won't!"

I don't want to promise anything, because if I were Rosa, I'd want to know that Mrs. McHenry secretly thinks the worst of me, just because of my race. Or would I? Would it make me feel uneasy every time I went to Margo's house? Would I still want to be friends with Margo if I knew she would lie about *me* to save Rosa?

Is ignorance really bliss or is it better to know the truth, even if it hurts?

"I won't tell her," I finally say, with great reluctance. "But don't ever do that again. To *either* of us."

"I won't," Margo says, but she doesn't sound very happy. And as we go our separate ways to class, I'm not sure if I believe her anyway.

As the morning goes on, I don't know if it's my imagination, but I feel like people are looking at me. I keep glancing down to check that I'm not wearing my breakfast on my vintage R.E.M. tee and my jeans are zipped, which they are. I even go into the bathroom in between classes to make sure that a disfiguring zit hasn't erupted on my face since I left the house this morning. But my skin is no more blemished than usual. When I walk to stats, Jamie Moss calls out to me, but he doesn't ask me for my homework.

"Sammy, hey! How's life treating you?"

"Okay, I guess."

"Are you sure?" he asks, the corner of his adorable mouth turning up.

"Um . . . yeah. How about you?"

"I'm good. We won three to zero over the weekend. You should have come," he says. "I'm starting to take it personally that you never come to see me play."

"Oh, it's not that. I just went to a concert on Saturday and then I had to catch up on homework and—"

"Yeah? Who'd you see?"

"Einstein's Encounter at the Bowery Ballroom."

"Never heard of them."

I guess Jamie isn't into indie bands.

"You should come to the next game. It's on Tuesday. Here."

"Definitely," I say, even though I have no idea if I can make it.

"Cool." Jamie grins and winks at me as we head to our respective desks.

I need to raise my prom asking odds.

Until Geneva Grady hands Jamie her cell phone and he looks at it, and the two of them exchange a glance and start whispering, shooting a look over at me as they do.

It feels like I'm walking around with a sign on my back that says something I really need to know, but it's written in Popular People, a language I don't speak.

It's not till I get to the media center for my open and bump into Noah that I'm finally clued into what's going on. He's wearing a particularly awesome Talking Heads T-shirt under a hunter-green flannel, which brings out that shade in his eyes.

"Hey, Noah," I say. "So what do you think of the Lighthouse Book Club selection? Did you start it yet?"

This month's book is M. L. Stedman's *The Light Between Oceans*. It's probably the most appropriately titled book we've ever read for the Lighthouse Book Club, given that the setting is a remote lighthouse off the coast of Australia.

"I like it so far," Noah says. "Although I can't imagine living on a lighthouse rock in the middle of nowhere. I mean, I've got no problem being alone if I've got good tunes and plenty of books to read. But not for months at a time—especially with no Internet!"

"I know what you mean," I say. "It would get lonely pretty quickly, I think."

Noah is regarding me with an oddly concerned expression. "Are you . . . doing okay?"

It's obvious he's not talking about the book anymore. The feeling of unease that I've been getting since I got to school blossoms into full-fledged panic.

"I would be if I knew why everyone keeps asking me that and looking at me funny."

Noah looks confused, and a slow flush rises from his neck up to his cheeks. "I . . . well . . . I mean . . ." Clearly unable to articulate, he pulls out his cell and points to the screen.

It takes my eyes a second or two to focus, but then I see the headlines on a news site: "New Territories Bank Corp Shares Plummet After Hacked Document Dump Reveals Sexism, Unequal Salaries, and Racism."

My lungs have forgotten how to work. *Breathe, Sammy, breathe.*

Everyone has something to hide, Sammy, Mom said.

But sexism? Unequal salaries? Racism?

"Sammy? Are you all right?"

The warmth of Noah's hand on my elbow brings me back to the media center. I take a deep, shuddering breath.

"I don't know," I whisper as I exhale, shakily. "I knew that my dad's company was hacked and the hackers said they were going to publish some of the documents today, but . . ."

Words collide in my head, but none of them are big enough to describe how I feel.

"Not that it was going to be this sensational?"

I slump into the nearest chair and let my backpack fall to the floor so I can cover my face with my hands and shut the world out. *Sensational* might describe the situation if your parent weren't involved. For me, though, it's like having the floor beneath my feet suddenly shatter into a million tiny fragments and disappear.

"I should probably read the story," I tell Noah. "Since it seems like everyone else has. And here I thought I was just being paranoid, but apparently not. It turns out everyone really *is* out to get me."

"Sammy, there's some stuff that's going to be hard to read," Noah warns. "Maybe you should wait till you get home."

"It'll be even worse if I read it at home," I tell him. "Besides, I need time to think about this before I see my parents."

"I get that," he says, but still looks worried. "I'll be over there if you need me."

I get onto the school computer and search for "New Territories Bank Corporation."

There are thousands of current hits.

The *Wall Street Journal* article focuses mainly on the drop in stock price, and whether that plus the security breach will cause Dad to lose his job. The *New York Times* article discusses the potential link between the mayor's decision to go in forcefully with riot police to clear the protesters and the timing of the data dump. The *Washington Post* says that a hack this size could only be the work of a foreign government and quotes the president as saying that such heinous cyber warfare cannot be allowed to go unpunished.

Wait, the president of the country is involved? Mom called this the Mother of All Monster Hacks, but it sounds like it's even bigger than that.

The *New York Post* headline is a sensational "Bank Corp Hacker Shocker!" Meanwhile, ZDNet, some business tech website, quotes an unnamed consultant who worked with New Territories Bank Corp, saying that the IT staff there were "clueless" and "comatose in the face of danger."

I live with one of the key players in this story and even I don't know the truth. In fact, I'm even more clueless than these reporters.

It's a very strange feeling to realize that you know so little about the life of a person you see every single day.

In the middle of all this, I get a text from Mom.

Maria is here. Did you borrow my metallic sweater without asking me? : /

Uh-oh. Now what do I do? I decide the safest course is to play dumb.

what sweater? why?

I just went to get another sweater and it fell out of the pile. It's two sizes smaller. I can't even wear it. It cost a fortune, too. AND a snagged thread in the back : /

it wasn't me!

It must have been Maria. She should know it was dry-clean only.

i guess it was her, then.

She swears on her son's life it WASN'T her.

I'm doing exactly the same thing Margo did, I realize, and I feel guilty about it, but not enough to tell my mom the truth and accept the consequences.

Like Mom said, everybody's got secrets they don't want the world to know.

i don't know, mom. GTG.

I wait, nervous to see if Mom responds, but she doesn't. I'm an awful person, but right now, relief outweighs remorse as I turn back to the news stories.

Jezebel has a front-page post with the headline "Bro Culture at New Territories Bank Corp."

It's about something two high-level executives at the bank called a female coworker in an email, while agreeing to offer her less than they would to a man in the same position. My dad is on the email. He doesn't call them out for the awful things they said, and even worse, he agrees to paying her less.

So wrong.

How can this be my dad, the one who tells me to work hard because if I do, "the sky's the limit"?

I don't even realize that I've put my head down until Noah asks, "Can I do anything?"

I lift my head. "I don't think so. I don't know. I don't know anything anymore."

"Maybe you should go home. I'm sure they'd understand—"

"No!" I insist. "Home is the last place I want to be right now."

"We've only got three more minutes left of open," Noah points out after a quick glance at the wall clock. "Do you want to skip out?"

I've never ditched class in my life. But the thought of going to science and seeing everyone stare at me now that I know why they're doing it is more than I can face.

"Yes. Please. Let's get out of here."

"Come on," he says. "We can go out the back of B wing. It's closest to where my car's parked."

You're supposed to sign out if you leave school. You need to have a note from the doctor or the dentist or provide the death certificate (seriously!) so they know that you and your parents aren't making stuff up. They don't even trust parents to tell the truth.

Now that I realize Dad's the CEO of Liar Inc., I can understand why.

A strong breeze whips around the corner of the building, and the door slams shut behind us, as if putting an exclamation point on my decision to cut class. `

"I've never done this before, ever," I confess to Noah as we walk briskly to his car.

"Me neither," he admits.

"Seriously? Why would you suggest it, then?"

He unlocks his car and gestures for me to get in. It's like sliding into a warm greenhouse after the wind outside.

"Because you looked like a caged animal on shelter death row that needed to be set free," Noah says, giving me a side-long look as he starts the car.

I start laughing, even though tears are welling in my eyes. Because it's the weirdest, sweetest thing that anyone has ever said to me.

Noah backs the car out of the space, then stops the car before pulling off. "Okay, that didn't come out right. In fact, it came out sounding all kinds of wrong."

"No, it was sweet," I tell him. "I *was* feeling kind of like a trapped shelter puppy."

"Phew!" he says, guiding the car out of the high school lot.

"Where do you want to go?" he asks.

"I don't know," I say. "Where do truants usually hang out?"

"Can we google that?" Noah asks. "Or maybe Siri knows."

We look at each other and crack up.

"We're so lame," Noah says. "We must be the lamest truants in the history of truancy."

"Pretty much," I agree. "That's what we get for being good little hamsters."

"Hamsters?"

"You know, running on our hamster wheels. Getting good grades and doing what we're supposed to do."

Noah laughs. "Yup, I'm a good hamster. But today, we're out of our cages. So where to, Hamster Girl?"

"Don't you mean Death Row Puppy?"

"Whatever. Just tell me where you want to go. Your wish is my command."

I think about and discard several options as too public. I don't want to go anywhere there's a risk of being seen and ratted out to my parents.

"What about the arboretum?" I say.

"Good thinking, Batman," Noah says, making a turn in that direction. "Not many people and plenty of camouflage."

"If I'm Batman, does that make you the Boy Wonder?" I ask.

Noah laughs. "I've always rather fancied myself as Alfred," he says in a pretty decent English accent. "The guy goes from hand-to-hand combat to computer programming to performing minor medical procedures to tending roses. Oh, and then he whips up a soufflé when he's done. That's hardcore."

"I'm down with having a butler," I say. "Having you as a chauffeur isn't bad, either."

"I just wish I were driving the Batmobile," Noah moans.

"At least you have your license," I point out. "And a car!"

"True," he agrees.

There are only two cars parked in the arboretum lot, and Noah and I don't recognize either of them. The trees provide shelter from the stiff breeze that's reminding us spring hasn't entirely sprung.

"Are you warm enough?" Noah asks. "Do you want my hoodie?"

"I'm okay, thanks."

We walk side by side along the trail in companionable silence. The pussy willow branches have sprouted their soft gray catkins. I stop to stroke them.

"I love pussy willows. They're so soft."

A woodpecker starts drumming suddenly in a nearby tree and it startles me.

"Little jumpy there, are we?" Noah says, putting a reassuring hand on my shoulder.

"Having the bottom drop out of your world will do that to you." I sigh, about to take another step down the trail, when he stops me and points up at a tree.

"Look," he whispers. "It's a robin."

The robin's burst of orange stands out against the leafless branch, making it easy to spot. It chirps, tilting its head, surveying us with one black eye.

"I've loved robins ever since reading *The Secret Garden*," I confess.

"Can't say I've read that one," Noah says.

"It's an oldie but goodie," I tell him. "Spoiler alert: A robin helps her find the key to the garden."

"Cool," Noah says.

We continue down the path, listening to the creaking of branches in the wind and different birdcalls. When we get to the stream, Noah stops to skip stones. He's pretty good at it. When I try, I can only get my stone to skip twice or three times, max, but he gets one to go six.

"How do you do that?" I ask, sitting down on a nearby log to watch his superior skill.

"Physics," he says. "This French physicist, Lydéric Bocquet, came up with the formula. It has to do with the stone's diameter, its velocity, mass, tilt, angle of attack, and the density of the water."

"Angle of attack, huh? That sounds fierce."

"It is! In World War II, the British designed a skipping bomb."

"What? You mean a bomb like a skipping stone? No way!"

"Way. I watched this old movie called *The Dam Busters*

with my grandpa. It was sick. They used the skipping bombs to destroy dams in Germany's industrial area."

"Was that one of your movie bonding things?"

He smiles. "You remembered." Picking up another rock, he slings it. Only four skips this time.

My phone buzzes. It's a text from Rosa: where are u?

"Confused is where I am," I mutter as I turn off my phone. I don't want to deal with the outside world right now.

Noah is crouched by the stream, looking for another perfect stone, but he looks up at me. The boy must have bat ears.

"That's understandable," he says.

"How can my dad have . . . He's not like that!" I say. "He's my dad. He's a good person."

I sound just like my mom. Ugh.

"You're his daughter, so he must have done *something* right," Noah says.

"I'm serious, Noah. My dad's not like that. The papers make him sound . . . awful. He's not."

Noah turns his gaze away to look at water bubbling over the rocks in the stream, and I wonder if he thinks I'm just a typical kid in denial about her dad.

Then he turns back and gestures for me to join him. I get up off the log and brush the bark off my butt, then go stand next to him.

"Okay, see that rock in the middle of the stream?" he asks, pointing.

"The green mossy one?"

He nods. Then, taking my hand and tugging, he leads me down the bank about ten paces.

"Okay, now look at it again from here."

It's so weird. From just a little way down the bank, the same rock looks different. It's gray brown rather than green, because the moss doesn't grow as much on this side.

"You wouldn't know it was the same rock from this angle," I say to Noah. "Are you doing this to distract me from my dad problems?"

He laughs. "No. I'm trying to help you find some perspective with your dad problems," he says. "Is it working?"

Then it dawns on me.

"Oh . . . So you're saying my dad can be a jerk and a good person at the same time?"

"Not a jerk, just—"

"But it's like two totally different people. How can you be two different people at the same time?"

"I don't know . . . maybe he's like Dr. Jekyll and Mr. Hyde?"

His wry delivery makes me laugh. It strikes me that Jamie probably wouldn't have made that joke. I feel like I'm cheating on my crush.

I wonder if Jamie would have offered to ditch with me. I doubt it. He wouldn't do anything to risk getting kicked off the lacrosse team.

A wood duck flies down from a nearby tree and lands in the river, making squealing noises, which are answered by a stuttering coo from up in the tree. It submerges its bright green head, searching for underwater edibles.

"I'm not exactly a big camping fan. In fact I hate it. But right now I'd rather stay here listening to the running water and the birds than go home to face a dad who suddenly feels like a stranger."

Noah tosses the stone he'd been holding in his other palm. It skips three times and then sinks to the bottom.

"Don't you think . . . maybe you should hear your dad out?" he says. "You know, give him a chance to explain?"

I don't really want to deal with this at all. I just wish this whole hacking thing would go away.

"I guess," I admit.

What I don't tell Noah is that even if my dad does explain, I'm not sure I believe him.

April 8

Noah dropped me back home at the usual time I'd get back from the bus.

"Here you go. Safely back at stately Wayne Manor," he said.

"Thanks, Alfred," I told him. "And not just for chauffeuring me."

"It was my pleasure," he said in his English accent, and the devilish smile made it seem like he really meant it.

Luckily, no one was home yet. The first thing I did was get online to read more about the hacked documents.

I thought it would help me understand, but it's just made me more upset and confused.

Which one is the real dad? The one I see and talk to at home or the one in the emails? It feels like they can't be the same person, even though they are both Dick Wallach, CEO of New Territories Bank Corporation. Noah's right. It is like freaking Jekyll and Hyde. I just hope that Jekyll Dad's still in there.

I asked my mom if there was anything in the hacked emails that might send Dad to prison. Besides being pissed that I'd even ask such a question, she said, "Your father is a good man." She's been saying that a lot lately. I wonder if she's trying to convince me or herself.

I've never thought of Dad as anything other than a good person. But as I read more emails, I start asking myself: What makes a person good?

There's one where the president of another company makes a joke about his Puerto Rican secretary "who lives in Spanish Harlem in an apartment with the illegal relatives she's brought over." Instead of telling him that's a horrible thing to say, Dad responds by making a snide comment about our cleaning lady, Maria, and her family.

I can't believe it. Maria is from Ukraine and she's worked really hard for our family for years. Sometimes she goes to another job at night after cleaning our house all day.

Then again, I was willing to sacrifice Maria to cover up my own lies. I guess maybe I inherited some of Dad's less awesome genes.

Just like Margo threw Rosa under the bus, letting her mom believe Rosa had been drinking at the concert because her mom thinks Rosa's a bad influence because of her skin color. And Rosa's our friend. My *best* friend.

Dad's stupid comment doesn't even make sense, because Maria is legal. One of the reasons she works so hard is because her son, Vasily, got straight As in community college and then transferred to the university. Now he's a senior and applying to law school.

To top it all off, it's so hypocritical, because we were immigrants, too. Not Mom or Dad or RJ or me. Not even my grandparents. But my great-grandparents were all the first generation to be born here, and their parents were just like Maria. So why is Dad making jokes about Maria when our family started out in this country in the same way?

The poem at the base of the Statue of Liberty says, "Give me your tired, your poor, your huddled masses yearning to breathe free." Where does it say anything about closing the door behind you so no other tired, poor, huddled masses can pass through it after you?

Is this the real American Dream? Everyone climbs the ladder of success and then pulls it up behind them so they can laugh, with all the other people who've made it, at those who are still jumping desperately to catch the bottom rung? Do they end up like Mrs. McHenry, automatically assuming that Rosa is trouble because she's from the latest nationality of immigrants being picked on?

If that's the way it is, maybe the people who were camping outside Dad's office are right to protest.

SIX

Mom looks awful when she gets home after work and picking up RJ from Photography Club. Her eye makeup is smudged and her hair is sticking up like she's spent the day trying to tear it out. Not that I blame her. I know the feeling. RJ gives me a warning glance as he heads to the refrigerator for a snack.

"Are you okay?" I ask. "You look kind of . . . rough."

"Not now, Sammy," she says in a quiet, even voice. She swings her bag off her shoulder and winces as it brushes her chest. "Ow."

"What?" I ask.

"Nothing," she says. "But I want to know why I got unexcused absence emails from your four afternoon classes."

Crap. Maybe I should have spent less time reading about Dad's emails and more time thinking of an excuse. Since I don't have an excuse, I go with the truth.

"People were staring at me at school all morning. I didn't

know why. And finally someone asked me if I was okay and I said I would be if it didn't feel like I was walking around with a Kick Me sign on my back and then he showed me some of the headlines."

"The ones about Dad?" RJ asks.

"Yeah. And I was so freaked out by them that I couldn't face going to school for the rest of the day. So I skipped out," I admit. "For the first time in my life, I'd like to point out."

"Running away from your problems is no way to solve them," Mom says. "This is going to be difficult, for all of us. For some time to come. You can't just cut class."

"Did Dad really say all the things the papers say he did?" RJ asks. "The stuff that was kind of racist and totally not PC?"

Mom doesn't answer. She just slumps into a kitchen chair and rubs her temples, like she's got a killer headache.

"'Cause if he did, that's so wrong," RJ continues. "Don't you always tell us we're supposed to accept people for who they are?"

Mom, who is usually so quick with answers, remains silent, her head in her hands.

"Mom," RJ persists.

"I heard you," she says, slowly raising her face. "I wish I knew what to say."

Most of the time, it annoys me that my parents think they have all the answers. But my mom admitting that she doesn't scares me.

"In theory, we're supposed to accept people for who they are," Mom says. "But once you get out into the world, life gets much more . . . complicated. There are pressures . . . You have to be part of a team . . . and—"

"That doesn't even make sense, Mom," I point out. "Like there aren't *pressures* in high school? Like you don't have to be *part of a team*? What are you even saying?"

"Sounds like a great big pile of grown-up bull to me," RJ says.

I stare at RJ, eyes wide, wondering what has gotten into him. He never talks this way, especially not to Mom.

She doesn't take it well.

"Okay, that's enough. I've had it. I need a Mom Time-Out. Go upstairs and do your homework."

"But *I* didn't do anything!" I protest.

"I don't care. Upstairs. *Now*."

RJ grabs his backpack and stomps out of the room, but I feel compelled to make a statement. "Fine, Mom. But I want to state for the record that you're being totally unfair."

"Get used to it, Sammy," Mom says, pulling out her phone. "*Life* is unfair."

It feels like she's saying that as much for her own benefit as for mine.

I turn on my heel and head for the stairs, but I stop half-way up when I hear Mom on the phone.

". . . And they're asking me questions that I can't answer,

Dick. It's not fair. You've got a work crisis, but we've got a crisis at home, too. More than one. I need you here."

And then I hear her losing it. Big-time. Not gentle, quiet crying. Loud, snorting sobs. I hesitate, torn between going down and putting my arms around her to offer comfort, and continuing upstairs to my room like I never heard anything.

I stand and listen to the heartbreaking sound of my mom's sobs for another minute, then quietly go up the rest of the stairs to my room and shut the door on her pain, the way she told me to.

My phone has been buzzing with texts the whole time, but clearly, family drama has been taking priority over everything today.

Two-thirds of them are from Rosa.

where were you today? did you skip out?

you must be wiggin! i am, kinda.

is all this stuff in the papers true?

where are you?

why aren't you answering me!

have you gone into the witness protection program?

will i ever see or talk to you again?

And then, ten minutes later:

are you dead?!! please tell me you're not dead!!!!

Witness Protection Program?! Wow, Rosa's been binge watching too many action movies again.

this is sammy's ghost. i regret to inform you that sammy is, in fact, dead. she says it was great knowing you.

also, now she doesn't have to worry about a date for prom.

My phone rings three seconds later.

"Oh my god, Sammy, I was fereeeeeeaaaaaaking out. How come you didn't answer any of my texts?"

"I don't know. I'm sorry. I guess . . ."

"Margo's been texting me to find out what's going on. She's worried, too."

"I don't have much to tell you. I'm just as confused as you are," I admit. "Helene's losing it completely and Dick's still at the office—which is pretty much the norm lately."

Rosa's quiet for a moment, then asks, "Do you think it's true, though? I mean . . . all the things they're saying on the news that he put in those emails? The . . . craptastic stuff?"

I don't want to believe it's true, but I saw the emails myself on the website where the hackers posted them. And I'm mortified, because Rosa's my best friend and she's Hispanic and my dad didn't call out his colleague who made a racist comment. He just went on to make one of his own. Is my dad no better than Margo's mom?

"I don't know."

"It just . . . seems so unlike your dad," Rosa says. "He's always so nice, and funny and polite. It just seems so . . . weird." She sounds sympathetic, but underneath, there's hurt and something else. Anger maybe? Which I could totally get. But I don't know how to talk to her about it. Not yet, anyway.

"Weird doesn't even begin to describe it. I feel like I don't even know Dick anymore. Like maybe he's not the same person I always thought he was."

"What, like now you find out he's the Dark Lord of Evil or whatever? *Sammy, I am your FATHER!*"

I have to laugh, because it's just so Rosa to go overboard. I might be freaked out and upset by some of the things that my dad supposedly said in those emails, but "Dark Lord of Evil" hadn't even crossed my mind.

"Or not. Maybe he just acts one way at home and a different way at work?"

"But . . . isn't that the same for everyone?" Rosa asks.

"What do you mean?"

"Well . . . you act one way around your parents and then totally different when you're with me," she explains.

"True," I concede. "And I guess even differently with some friends than we do with others, too."

"Exactly! Like I can make fart jokes with you, but Margo thinks they're gross and stupid."

"Promise me you will never get mature enough to think that fart jokes are gross and stupid," I beg Rosa.

"I promise that when we are ancient crones sitting in rocking chairs in our nursing home, I will keep you amused with fart jokes," Rosa says. "That's if I don't get Alzheimer's and forget everything like my poor *abuelo*."

"I feel so much better now," I tell her.

"Do you? Really?" she asks.

The truth is, I don't know how I feel. I won't know that till I can talk to my dad.

"Yeah," I lie. "Except . . . does that mean I have to start worrying about a date for the prom again? Because Ghost Sammy enjoyed not having to think about it."

"Yup. And APs. And taking your road test next week."

"Good thing there's such a relaxed atmosphere here at home," I say, pushing the irony pedal to the metal.

"Ha! Well, at least you still have your sense of humor," Rosa says.

"Yeah. I guess there is that."

Cue awkward pause. There's an elephant on the phone between us, one that neither of us seems willing or able to name.

"Well, *hasta la vista*," Rosa says.

After she hangs up, I stare at my cell, wondering how long things will be awkward between us. I wonder if Mom's stopped crying, and if Dad's on his way home yet. But most of all, I wonder if life will ever go back to normal again. Since I don't have answers to any of those questions, I put on the Einstein's Encounter channel and do the one thing I'm good at, which is drilling for the APs. At least if my future ends up being totally destroyed, no one can say it's for lack of studying.

Dad finally gets home at like nine thirty. Noah told me to give him a chance to explain, but pretty much as soon as he walks in the door, my dad calls us downstairs. RJ is already half-asleep, but Dad shouts up that he needs to come down anyway, because it's important.

This sounds ominous, not like a *Hey, let's have a cozy chat about this situation* thing. Not only that, we don't get called into the family room but the "formal living room" with its stiff-backed armchairs, the World's Most Uncomfortable Sofa (TM), and the antique coffee table we're not allowed to put our feet on, even when we're not wearing shoes.

Ominous and ominous-er.

Mom has stopped crying, but her eyes are red-rimmed and she's twisting a bunch of tissues nervously with her fingers. Dad looks even worse than he did yesterday, something I wouldn't have thought possible twenty-four hours ago. You'd never know this was the same guy who looked so confident and in control on the cover of *Fortune* six months ago as "The Bold Face of American Banking" (whatever that means). He's sitting in the biggest armchair, the one we jokingly called the Throne, like he's about to dispense some medieval justice.

"Sit down, kids. We need to talk," he says.

As I take a seat next to RJ on the World's Most Uncomfortable Sofa (TM), I wonder if there's ever been a time in the history of parenting when the kids are ushered into the most ornately furnished room in the house and told, "We need to talk," and it ends well. The probability of that is zero, and I wonder what new ax Dad's about to lower on our heads.

"There's been some developments with the hacking situation," Dad says. "And this time, it involves you."

"What do you mean, involves us?" I ask.

Mom twists the tissues in her hands even tighter. If they were someone's neck, that someone would be a goner.

"What I mean is that the hackers targeted us personally," Dad explains. "Well, specifically *me* personally, but in doing so, you were caught in the net."

RJ and I look at each other. I can tell he's just as clueless about what Dad means as I am.

"Caught in what net?" I ask. "What are you talking about?"

"What I'm talking about is that they targeted me at home," Dad says. "Which only goes to show how unscrupulous these people are."

"But what did they do?" RJ asks. "And what does it have to do with Sammy and me?"

"They hacked our cloud backup," Dad says. "And—"

"But how could they do that?" RJ interrupts. "Don't we have a firewall? I thought that guy from Geekify put one in."

"Geekitude," I correct him. "Yeah, at the same time he set it up so all of our devices 'seamlessly sync to the cloud.'"

"Firewall, schmirewall," Mom mutters.

"It had nothing to do with the firewall," Dad says, like he's writing a chapter in *Hacking for Dummies*. "The problem was with cloud backup protocols. Because there's so much publicly available information about me, they were able to request a password reset and get onto our backup that way. It's what's known as social engineering."

I hear RJ asking Dad what this means, but I am already frozen with horror because I think i already know: that they have everything that is on my laptop and my phone. Pictures. Emails. Texts . . .

"Oh my god!" I start shaking when I realize the worst part of all. "They have my *diary*."

"You keep a diary?" RJ asks. He sounds disappointed that he's missed an opportunity to find dirt on me that could be used as leverage to get me to give him stuff or drive him places when I get my license.

"Yeah. I *thought* I was being smart by keeping it on my laptop so you couldn't snoop in my room to find it."

My parents don't seem to be paying attention to me. They're too busy exchanging pointed looks at each other. My mom appears as if she might detonate at any second. Dad gives her a heated stare and shakes his head slightly, like he's warning her to keep her finger off the red button.

"What else does the 'seamless sync to the cloud' back up?" RJ asks.

"Everything on your phone and your laptop," Dad says.

"What, you mean my *texts*?" RJ is finally catching on to just how awful this is.

Dad nods.

"And pictures? And chats?"

"All of it," Dad says.

"But that's not fair!" RJ says. "How can they do that? That's our personal private stuff!"

"If these hackers don't care about breaking the law, what makes you think they give two hoots about our privacy?" Mom snarls, and it's hard not to feel like her rage is directed at us as well as at them.

"They don't," Dad says in a slow, even voice. "This is a malicious act of vandalism, and the FBI is investigating. But in the meantime, we have to deal with the fallout. CodeRed, our crisis communications company, which is already working with us to respond to the corporate hack, is going to help us manage our way through this hack of our personal systems as well."

"What do you mean *manage our way*?" I ask.

"He means stick to the script," Mom says. "And do as you're told."

"What script?" RJ asks. "I don't get it. Do *what* as we're told?"

"I need your phones and laptops until I've had a computer-security expert go over the home situation," Dad says.

"What?!" RJ explodes.

"This is a joke, right?" I say at the same time.

"Trust me, this is the furthest thing from a joke I have ever said to you," Dad says. "Do you kids understand the gravity of this situation?"

"Do *you* understand that I have AP exams starting in three weeks? How am I supposed to study if I can't use my computer?"

Playing the high-stakes-tests card gets Dad's attention. I watch my parents. At times like this, it pays off.

He looks to Mom for assistance, but she gives him a *This is your mess, get yourself out of it* look and examines her fingernails like the condition of her nail polish is her number one priority in this time of crisis.

"Uh . . . you can go to the library. They have computers there. Study at the library. Either stay after school or go to the public library."

"But, Dad—"

"It'll only be for a day or two, until I can get the security consultant here," Dad says in a tone that tells me not to argue. "And I *don't* want you going onto any of the hacker sites that post those documents. Do I make myself clear?"

"Crystal clear," I mutter.

"Clear as mud," RJ complains. "This sucks. It's so unfair."

"Who ever said life was *fair*?" Dad asks.

"You guys did!" RJ shouts. "You said we had to share, otherwise it wasn't fair. You said to tell the truth, otherwise it wasn't fair. You told us to accept people for who they are, or else it's not fair. You always tell us to do the right thing, otherwise it isn't fair. And now it turns out you're nothing but a bunch of h-hypocrites!"

His voice breaks on the last word, and he gets up and storms out of the room.

"RJ, get back here!" Dad shouts after him, but it doesn't do any good. A minute later, my brother's door slams with such ferocity the chandelier in the hallway tinkles.

My brother's idea of payback is still primitive. But he's young. There's time for him to refine it.

Dad looks at me, his lips compressed into a thin line of not very well concealed frustration.

"I trust I can count on you to behave in a more mature and rational manner, Sammy."

I think of all the things that I want to ask him. About the

things I saw in those emails that made me wonder if he's been lying to me all this time. But as Mom said, everyone has secrets. And when my parents find out mine, I'm dead.

"Sure, Dad. No problem," I assure him.

I can still pretend I'm a good kid. Even if my cover is about to be blown to smithereens.

April 8

One H-bomb detonated. Who knows what'll be waiting at school.

I can't believe this is happening. The APs are in three weeks and I can't use my laptop or my cell phone. This is my future we're talking about.

I had to dig out this Hello Kitty diary with a tiny little lock and key that Uncle Kenny and Aunt Cindy gave me for Chanukah when I was seven. The last entry was "Mom and Dad said they're going to take me to the American Girl store for tea for my birthday! Rosa went and they give you a teapot and tea set for your doll, too. I'm saving my money to buy Coconut, the American Girl dog, because Mom and Dad won't let me get a real dog. ☹"

Scruffles and I just had a laugh about that. I told him that I bought Coconut, but a stuffed dog is no substitute for the real thing, no matter how cute and fluffy it is. I never gave up nagging my parents and they gave in two years later.

"And that's when we got you, and lived happily ever after until hackers threatened to post all our private stuff on the Internet," I told Scruffles, who wagged his tail and licked my face, looking like he was grinning, with his tongue hanging out the side of his mouth.

I ripped that page out and tore it into little pieces because it reminded me how upset I was when it turned out Dad had to go give a Really Important Speech in Paris on my birthday and Mom was invited. She wasn't about to give up an all-expenses-paid trip to Paris for tea at the American Girl store. Sure, I still got to go have tea with my doll, but it was with Grandma Sally and Grandpa Marty, not my parents. Maybe I shouldn't be so upset—I mean, there are kids who would kill for the chance to take their doll for tea at the American Girl store, no matter who took them. But at the time, I felt totally betrayed that it wasn't my parents. They'd promised me we'd go together. It felt like they didn't love me as much as they loved work and expenses-paid travel.

Guess I should have learned the lesson when I was seven. "Life's not fair, Sammy." People break promises, even the ones you trust to tell you the truth. Stuff happens.

Seeing my ill-formed seven-year-old handwritten hope made me mad and hurt all over again, but that disappointment seems lame now.

What if the hackers put my diary online? How will I ever be able to show my face at school again? I mean, all those long ramblings about Jamie Moss. I could DIE. And the probability calculations about if he'll ask me to prom? What about the things I wrote about Rose and Margo. UGH! My life is over. Seriously, it's ruined before I've even got my driver's license. How sad is that?

I might throw up.

It's one thing to be a weird geek in private, when you think no one's going to see it. Then it's just part of what makes you awesome—a secret identity and all. It's another to have your innermost thoughts posted for everyone in your high school—or even the world—to see. Literally, THE WORLD.

And what about my parents? Dad said we can't read the stuff the hackers post, but does the same go for them? Because if they read my texts and my diary, I'm done for. They'll know that I went to the concert. They'll know that I lied. I'll be grounded for life before I can say: "You've been hacked."

SEVEN

"Sammy!" Rosa shouts as soon as I get off the bus. "What's up with you? I've been texting you all morning and you haven't answered!"

I don't want to shout why where everyone can hear. "Hold on, I'm coming over."

I make my way through the knots of kids hanging out, till I get over to where Rosa is standing with Margo. Margo gives me a warning look, but I'm not going to say anything. I've got enough stress without stirring things up between my friends.

"Are you pretending to be dead again?" Rosa says. "Because it's getting really old."

She sounds mad at me. Great. Margo's the one she *should* be mad at, not me.

"No! It's not my fault, Rosa. Really. Dick quarantined my phone and my laptop."

"Oh crap. Did your parents find out you went to the Einstein's Encounter concert?" Margo asks.

"Not yet," I say. "At least not that I know of."

"So how come you've got a complete device ban, then?" Rosa asks.

I look around to make sure no one is listening.

"It's the hackers," I explain, so quietly that they have to lean in to hear me. "They managed to hack onto our family cloud. And they're threatening to post that stuff, too. I might die waiting for the impending Sammypocalypse."

"But why? You don't work for the bank!" Rosa exclaims. "That's crazy!"

"Keep it down," I hiss. "I don't want everyone to know. It's bad enough having to worry that my deepest private thoughts might be posted online at any minute."

"What do you mean your 'deepest private thoughts'?" Margo asks.

"Oh, Sammy . . ." Rosa groans. "You kept an online journal?"

"It wasn't *online*. It was one hundred percent *off*line," I insist. "It's quicker to type than write."

"That's true," Margo agrees.

"Plus, that way I didn't have to worry about my parents or RJ finding a diary in my room and reading it," I continue. "What I *didn't* count on was Dick and the Geekitude guy and their '*seamless backup to the cloud.*'"

"What's the potential damage?" Rosa asks, getting straight to the bottom line. "I mean, on a scale of one to ten, how bad is it if they do post it?"

"I'm thinking . . . ELEVEN?" I say. "I feel sick just thinking about it."

"That's bad," Margo says. "Really bad."

Like I hadn't figured that out already.

"What kind of things are we talking about?" Rosa asks.

"Well, let's see . . . a probability tree involving prom, Jamie Moss, and yours truly. That alone is enough to sign my social death warrant."

"You *made a probability chart about a guy asking you to the prom?*" Margo says, starting to crack up. "Really? Sammy, you're an even bigger nerd than everyone says you are!"

I am not amused. "People say I'm a nerd? Like *who* exactly?"

"It doesn't matter what a few idiots think, Sammy," Rosa says. "You've got bigger problems to deal with." She glares at Margo. "We're supposed to be *supportive* right now," she reminds her.

"My student government friends aren't idiots, Rosa," Margo says, lifting her chin. "But *whatever*. Sorry, Sammy."

Rosa ignores her.

There's an undercurrent between them and they haven't even read my journal. I feel a burst of panic when I think about how much worse it will be when they do.

"So what else?" Rosa asks. "Did you write about the concert? Could your parents find out?"

"Of course I wrote about the concert. It's my journal!" I say. "And I wrote about the sweater and the puke and it shrinking and Helene blaming Maria."

"This isn't an eleven," Rosa groans. "It's a twelve."

"More like a twenty," Margo says in a funereal tone. "If your parents read that, you're going to be grounded until you go to college. Maybe even *in* college."

If my friends are trying to make me feel better, they're failing. Epically.

"Well, now that we've ascertained that I'm a Dead Girl Walking, I might as well walk to class for a final day before the crap *really* hits the fan."

"When will that happen?" Rosa asks as we start heading into the building.

I shrug. "Your guess is as good as mine," I tell her. "That's *if* it happens. Maybe my dad will pay them off. Maybe the FBI will catch the hackers before they can post anything. Maybe the earth will be hit by an asteroid and posting the innermost thoughts of a teenage girl, as awesome as she is, will seem pointless compared to survival. I can live in hope."

"I wouldn't hold your breath waiting for the asteroid," Margo says. "Neil deGrasse Tyson says that the next time there's a possibility of that is in 2029. And even then, it's supposed to miss."

I stare at her. "And you're calling *me* a nerd?"

"Knowing when the earth could be potentially annihilated qualifies as self-preservation, not nerdiness," Margo says matter-of-factly.

I look to Rosa for a ruling as a neutral party.

"I'm pleading the Fifth," she says. "But it's *definitely* walking a fine line."

We head in different directions for first period. I'm so busy contemplating my potential doom that I'm halfway to my class before I realize I'm behind Jamie Moss and his friends Pete O'Doule and Daryl Williams and that they're talking about prom. Specifically, Daryl just asked Jamie: "When are you going to ask her?"

To my frustration, he doesn't reveal the identity of "her."

I slow down so I'm far enough behind to still hear them, but not close enough that my presence is obvious. If I have to drop out of high school due to Sammygeddon, maybe these talents will come in useful in my backup career as a spy.

"I'm thinking Thursday before school starts," Jamie says. "My older brother said I should get on it because girls need time to pick out dresses and stuff. I was going to do it tomorrow, but we've got a game tonight and I've got to get the goods for the ask."

"You're assuming she'll say yes," Peter says.

Jamie punches his arm. "Of course she's going to say yes. She totally wants me."

I stop, pretending to tie a shoelace on my shoes—which don't have laces—and let them continue down the hall.

She totally wants me.

Is it me he's talking about? I mean, yeah, I totally DO want him to ask me to prom, but . . . wanting to go to a dance with him and wanting *him* are two different things. At least in the way I think he means.

Except I don't even know if it's me he's talking about because I don't know if I'm the one he's planning on asking.

Then I realize that if the hackers include my diary in their data dump, Jamie's going to know exactly how desperate I've been for him to ask me.

On the upside, at least I'll finally know if I'll be Jamie's prom date. On the downside, I think I might vomit.

When I see Margo and Rosa in the hallway between classes, I tell them what I overheard.

"What do you think?" I ask.

Margo is suddenly deeply fascinated by something on the ceiling over my right shoulder. But Rosa looks me in the eye. "Sammy, I don't think he's going to ask you. He hasn't shown any signs of being interested."

"Yes, he has," I protest. "He talks to me in class and he's asked me to come to his games. You think Eddy Lau is going to ask you because you talk in class."

"I know, but Eddy also . . . He . . . Well, he's shown he likes me that way," Rosa says. "Not at first. Gradually. And Jamie . . . he's . . . I just don't see it."

"But you're not in class with us! Of course you don't see it."

Why are my friends being like this, when I always support them about everything?

Margo finally stops dissecting the ceiling tiles with her eyes, but it's to join Rosa in raining on my parade.

"I might not see him with you, Sammy, but I see him flirting with everyone else," she says. "I don't even get why you like him. Okay, so he's totally hot, but he's a jerk. Does that remind you of your dad or something?"

Some things, once uttered, cannot be unheard or unsaid. Also, EW.

Even though Rosa tells Margo she's out of line, I turn and walk away without a word, knowing that she just fired a massive torpedo into the hull of our friendship.

I don't know if the damage can be repaired.

I curl my feelings up into a tight ball and hide it away so I can walk through the hall with outer shell intact, like nothing is wrong. *Never give in, never give in, never, never, never,* even if you feel like an extra in George Romero's *Night of the Living Dead.* Just shuffle your zombie body from one class to the next, trying not to think—except academically of course, because you still have to get good grades for college and that prize job at which some guy like your dad will probably end up making sexist jokes about you and paying you less than a man for doing the same job.

I slump into my chair in AP English, without even saying hi to Noah, who's already sitting at the desk behind me. Looking adorkable in a T-shirt that says "Physics is Phun," I can't help but notice despite my impending doom.

"Who died?" Noah asks.

"My social life," I utter in a monotone.

"Look at the bright side," he says. "At least you had one to begin with."

"I'm having a hard time seeing the bright side of anything right now."

"What happened?" he asks. "Is it the stuff in the papers about your dad?"

"That's just the tip of the misery iceberg. Ninety percent of it is still underwater," I confess. "At least until the hackers decide to post it."

"There's more to come out about your dad?"

"Not just about him," I reveal, before realizing I shouldn't have.

But Noah's going to find out soon enough. Chances are, everyone will. How am I going to face school when that happens?

Noah looks confused, but he can't ask me any more questions, because class starts. Except I feel a warm, gentle tap on my shoulder, and he passes me a note.

What do you mean, "not just about him"? What's going on? Are you okay? You seem really bummed.

My pen hesitates over the scrap of paper. The feeling ball is threatening to come unraveled, and I can't let that happen. But I have to talk to someone, and so far my best friends are failing miserably.

They hacked our family cloud backup. Targeting my dad, but the rest of us are collateral damage. So pretty soon, my entire life might go viral for the entire school's viewing pleasure.

I refold the note and then, as soon as Ms. Brown's back is turned, pass it to Noah. He returns it pretty quickly.

Wow, no wonder you look so bummed. I wish I knew what I could do to help, but even Alfred Pennyworth is at a loss on this one.

I swallow the lump rising in my throat as I write quickly. I know it's an unfair thing to ask, but I pass the note back to him.

Can you promise not to hate me?

I wait for an answer, but there's no tap on my shoulder.

I can't blame him. Who in their right mind would make a promise like that when they don't even know what truths might come out about me?

Still, it hurts. Just like everything else.

#Irony

When the bell rings, I grab my books and try to escape class without facing Noah. But just outside the classroom door, I hear "Sammy, wait!" and feel a hand on my shoulder.

Stiffening, I turn.

"Why would you think I'd *hate* you?" Noah asks, looking so genuinely confused it's almost comical. "Am I going to read that Batman steals candy from kindergartners for kicks or something?"

No, but you are going to read that I've been calculating the probability of Jamie Moss asking me to the prom, and wonder why you were ever nice to me.

"Who, me?" I pause and then continue with gallows humor: "No, this Caped Crusader is too worried about getting cavities. Now, ice cream, on the other hand . . . that's fair game."

"Oh, that's okay," Noah says, totally deadpan. "Ice cream is nectar from the gods. Especially the stuff from that new place, Lickety Splits."

A spark of life flickers in my zombie heart, and a giggle escapes my lips, met by Noah's answering smile.

"It's good to know that we see eye to eye on this," I say.

"You can always count on me to back you up," Noah says.

"Well, thanks," I tell him, and I'm not talking about stealing ice cream from kindergartners, because I really never would, and I know Noah wouldn't, either.

"I mean it, Sammy," he says, and he's serious now, too. He flashes me a wide grin and I feel a small burst of happiness.

But it can't possibly last.

Because of my computer lockdown at home, I stay in the library after school to study, which really does make me feel like a nerd. At least at home I'm studying in private, but here there's no hiding it. And it turns out I'm not the only one.

"I can't believe there are so many people here after school," I say to Ms. Stephens, the media specialist. "I thought the media center would be dead."

"We're busy most days after school," she tells me. "Not all our students have their own laptops. A lot of our kids don't have any computer at home at all."

And here I was feeling sorry for myself because I can't use my laptop for a few days. I can't even imagine not having one at all. Dad always tells us that NTBC pays for the privileges we enjoy. But what if the protesters have a point?

I'm sitting here in the school library trying to cram all these facts into my head for the AP Government exam, but I feel like all this information I've been working so hard to learn isn't telling me what I really need to know.

Because what I really need to know is not on a standardized test.

How do I figure out what the truth is and what's lies? I'm starting to wonder if the people I've always trusted to tell me the truth have only been telling me part of it. Maybe the people who are breaking the law could help me to discover the rest.

I start to google "New Territories Bank Corp hack," but then close the browser window. What if I find out more things that freak me out? What if what I read just ends up shattering the foundations of my world even more?

You're here to study for APs. Remember: College. Your Future. Study, Sammy, study.

I spend the rest of the time, till my mom picks me up, taking practice tests. Even though the rest of my life is a mess, I do well on these.

April 9

Mom is late to pick me up. Figures. I can't wait to get my license.

Today's Headline: Jamie Moss is going to ask someone to the prom on Thursday. The Million Dollar Question is: Will he ask me?

There are several new factors to consider when assessing the probability of this occurring.

The biggest one, of course, is whether the hackers post my ENTIRE LIFE ONLINE in the next 48 hours, which is a pretty big wild card. If they don't, then my old probability charts might still stand.

But on the other hand, maybe not. Going with AN Other would be a lot more appealing at this point if that AN Other happened to be named Noah Woods.

So I guess there are two new probabilities to figure out: if the hackers don't post my diary before Jamie asks, and if they do. In both scenarios, I'm going to assume that AN Other is Noah. Not that I know he would ask me. But . . . I think I'd like it if he did. I guess I could always ask someone myself. #GirlPower, right?

I've changed my preferences for Jamie because . . . well, I'm not as sure he's as highly preferred as an option, especially if AN Other is Noah. I'm making him 60% vs. 40% for Noah, rather than 80% vs. 20% for unnamed other.

Based on the evidence of how he smiles at me, the concern he showed when I was upset, and how he was willing to cut class for the very first time in his Hamster Boy life to make me feel better and play Alfred to my Batman, I think there's just as good a probability of Noah asking me as random AN Other—assuming the data dump doesn't happen anytime soon. So based on that, here's how it looks:

After Hack Prom Decision Tree*

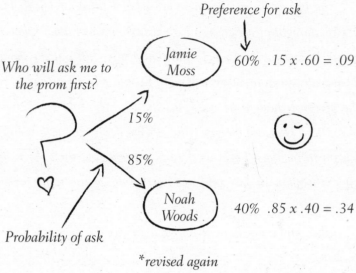

Preference for ask

Who will ask me to the prom first?

Jamie Moss   60%   .15 x .60 = .09

15%

85%

Noah Woods   40%   .85 x .40 = .34

Probability of ask

*revised again

Well, that's interesting. The numbers tell me Noah is a better bet. Which is really strange because I've been dreaming about Jamie asking me for so long. Weird.

Still, there's the HUGE variable that must be considered—namely, if the hackers decide to include my diary in their next document dump. If that happens, then how would it affect the likelihood of Jamie Moss asking me to prom? I mean, he'd *inevitably see the previous probability trees I created on this very subject. UGH!!!!!!!!!! I want the ground to open up and swallow me just thinking about it.*

It could reinforce his opinion that "she totally wants me." But if I'm not the she in question, I'm doomed to a life of total and complete mortification, forever. As for Noah, he might think . . . I can't even.

The biggest irony? I'm not sure what I think or I feel. I've always thought of myself as a logical person, but I don't know if numbers and logic can help me figure this stuff out anymore. That worked before, when I thought I could rely on my dad to be the person I thought he was. He's the guy who told me: "Logic never lies." He's also the guy who tells me I can achieve anything I want to in life if I just work hard enough, but then agrees to offer a woman in his company less for doing the same job as a man.

Logic might not lie, but people do. Even the ones you love.

eIGHT

Mom hasn't exactly been a ray of sunshine lately, but she looks particularly grim when she finally pulls up to the front of school. I feel like I've been waiting forever. I'm barely in the passenger seat before she launches in on me.

"I'm going to ask you a question, Samantha Wallach, and I want you to answer me very carefully," Mom says as she pulls away from the curb with a very uncharacteristic screeching of tires.

Uh-oh. This can't be good. Use of one's full name by a grim-faced parent means trouble. Add the sudden fondness for the gas pedal and we're talking *big* trouble.

Maybe I should have walked home when I had the chance.

"Did you borrow my silver sweater without asking me? The one you assured me previously you did not borrow, and that I accused Maria of washing and shrinking?"

Busted. Double down on the lie, or fess up?

The few seconds I take to think about it is enough of an answer for Mom.

"Don't bother. I have my answer. I know you lied about it, and I also know you went to that concert your father and I specifically told you was a no-go without an adult chaperone."

I grip the door handle, trying to prevent full-on panic. "What do you mean, *you know*?"

Mom slams on the brakes at the red light so hard that my head almost hits the dash, even though I'm wearing my seat belt.

"I *mean* that, thanks to the hackers, I've had the opportunity to peruse your diary. And let me tell you, it made *eye-opening* reading."

I feel sick to my stomach. "They posted my diary online? And you read it? It's private!"

"Yes, I did. And I know that you lied to us."

"How could you read my diary? That's so wrong, Mom! Who do you think you are, the NSA?"

"It's not private anymore, Samantha," Mom retorts. "Don't try to change the subject."

"I'm not trying to change the subject, Mom, I'm trying to find out if I'm ever going to be able to face going back to school in this lifetime. How could you do that? You had no right to read it! I can't believe they actually posted my diary. So, like, *anyone* can read it?"

Please say no. Please say this is all just a really bad prank you and Dad are playing on me for some reality show and the host is about to pop out from the backseat and say, "AHAHAHAHA, just kidding! Aren't your parents such jokesters?"

No such luck.

"Not just your diary. Our entire private life is an open book," Mom says, acid lacing every word. "Why did I ever give up my Filofax?"

I don't know what a Filofax is, or why Mom misses hers. I just keep hearing *Our entire private life is an open book*, and feel acid in the back of my throat. "Stop the car, I'm going to throw up," I say urgently.

"I don't have time for your drama right now, Sammy," Mom snaps.

"I mean it, Mom!"

She glances over, sees me gagging, and pulls into the right lane, cutting off a landscaper's truck and narrowly avoiding hitting it. The driver leans on the horn, and Mom tells him where he can go as she hits the curb and stops, flicking on her blinkers.

"Quick, outside," she says.

I manage to fling the door open and throw up a granola bar and bile onto the sidewalk.

But as I lean over, panting, feeling my head and stomach spinning in different directions, I know that this feeling of relief is only temporary.

The worst is yet to come.

Apparently puking convinces Mom that I'm not simply being a drama queen and she doesn't just lay off for the rest of the ride home, she actually shows concern for my health and well-being, putting a hand on my forehead and neck to check if I have a fever (according to the hand-mometer my temperature reads normal) and pouring me a glass of regular ginger ale (not diet, because I need to replace my sugar) when we get home. But once she's determined that my stomach has settled and I've got a bit of color in my cheeks, it's back to the lecturing.

She doesn't realize that even though I'm not trembling anymore, I'm still reeling from anxiety. My journal is online. Private thoughts no one was ever supposed to see. Anyone with an Internet connection can look straight into my brain.

I think I'm going to throw up again.

Mom sits down in the chair opposite from where I'm lying on the sofa and looks me in the eye.

"So, Samantha. You've been lying to us. To me."

I swallow the bile that's rising again in my throat. What can I say? There's no use pretending I didn't. Besides, my face, which I can feel flushing, provides the icing on the proof cake.

"Yeah, and the only reason you know that is because you read my private journal. You violated my Fourth Amendment protections against unreasonable search and seizure."

"I didn't," Mom points out. "The hackers did. I just read what they posted."

"Which you told us not to do," I reply, feeling vindicated anyway.

"You can try playing the lawyer, Samantha, but it doesn't change the fact that you lied to your parents. And that has consequences."

I realize that even though I'm mad about Mom invading my privacy, she's not going to be the only one, and at this point, maybe being apologetic is the wiser strategy.

"I'm sorry, Mom."

"Sorry you lied, or sorry you got caught?" Mom asks.

Of course I'm sorry I got caught. If it wasn't for those hacker jerks, I wouldn't have been. Did they not realize they were ruining my life?

"What's the difference?" I ask. "I'm sorry, okay?"

"There's a big difference, Sammy. I know you wouldn't lie thinking you'd get caught. You're too smart for that."

Is it a sign of how messed up and insecure I am that I'm happy Mom's telling me I'm smart when she's in the middle of lecturing me for lying?

"You would have gotten away with it if not for this hacking nightmare," Mom says, her shoulders slumped as if from the burden of contemplating it. I know how she feels. "But you didn't just lie about going to the concert. That would have been bad enough. You also lied about borrowing—and ruining—my sweater."

"I know."

"Do you realize I accused Maria? That innocent hardworking woman who has been cleaning up your messes for over five years? And you knew all along that you were the one who had done it and you let her take the blame?" Mom's voice is rising in pitch and volume, and so are my feelings of guilt. "What if I'd fired her?"

"You would have *fired Maria* over a *sweater*?"

"Would you have told the truth if I had?"

Would I have? It would have meant owning up to the bigger lie. Would I have done it to save Maria's job?

The look on my face must give me away.

"You're not sorry for lying, Sammy. Not yet. Being sorry means feeling remorse," Mom says. "And then there's the trust issue. How are we supposed to trust you from now on?"

"I've been totally trustworthy my entire life until now," I protest. "So now, because of one screwup, you're never going to trust me again?"

"Exactly right," Mom says, nodding. "I'm afraid to break it to you, Sammy, but that's how trust works. It takes a long time to build it and not a lot to destroy it. That's why you're grounded."

"What?"

"You heard me. Until after the SAT. And you're going to have to pay for a new sweater."

She's joking, right? I can't even imagine how much that sweater cost. But even worse . . .

"You're not serious. What about prom?"

Assuming I have a date, that is. And assuming I can ever show my face at school again.

"Including prom."

Unreal. It can't be happening.

"Prom's the only thing I've got to look forward to. I might as well just die now." Which doesn't sound like a terrible idea when you think about it. I won't have to go to school tomorrow. Or ever again.

Mom takes a deep unsteady breath.

Smart move, Sammy. You just pushed her into ballistic mode.

"Death isn't a joking matter, Samantha," she snaps. Her hand is shaking on the arm of the chair. "And if you were looking forward to prom so much, maybe you should have thought twice before breaking the rules."

"You know why I decided to break the rules?" I tell Mom as I get off the sofa, fueled by anger just as big as hers. "Because you're so irrational and unfair!"

Maybe it's childish, but I stomp up the stairs, trying to make scuff marks on the hardwood floor because I know that will drive my parents crazy. But so what? They're driving me crazy. You try so hard to be a good kid all your life, and then do one thing wrong and all of a sudden you're the devil's spawn, grounded until after the SAT and banned from prom.

I can't even text or email my friends until Dad gets home with the security expert later tonight. They're too busy cleaning up the mess at the office to worry about my lack of communication devices. So I don't know yet—did Rosa and Margo read my journal, too? Do they hate me for things I wrote? Do they hate each other?

Even though I'm afraid of what I'd find, it's just making things worse that I can't go online to assess the damage from having the contents of my brain cyber-spilled.

RJ comes into my room two minutes after I throw myself on the bed to sulk, Scruffles at his heels.

"I can't believe you're grounded for so long," he says.

As if I needed reminding.

"Leave. Now."

Scruffles' tail stops wagging at my harsh tone.

"Not you, Scruffulicious," I croon. "*You* can stay."

My goofy voice convinces Scruffles it's safe to jump on the bed and curl up.

"What did you do, rob a bank?" RJ asks.

"If I robbed a bank, I'd be sitting on a beach sipping virgin coladas, not stuck in my room answering your stupid questions."

RJ plunks down next to Scruffles. "Or you'd be in jail."

"Details. By the way, I told you to *leave*, not sit down and make yourself comfortable."

"I don't think it's fair that Mom read your diary when they made *us* promise not to read anything."

I sit up to make sure the pillow didn't impede my hearing. "Seriously? You don't think it's fair?"

"Do you?" he asks.

"Of course not! But I didn't think *you'd* care."

"Why wouldn't I?" RJ looks confused and . . . offended even?

"I don't know. If you want to know the truth, sometimes I get the impression that you like when I get in trouble."

RJ buries his face in Scruffles' coat. His back heaves. He's not . . . *crying*, is he?

But then he lifts his head suddenly and his face is flushed red, and he's . . . grinning?

"If you want to know the truth, yeah, sometimes I do love it when you get in trouble," he confesses. "It's fun to see Perfect Big Sister fall off her pedestal once in a while."

"Perfect Big Sister!" I snort. "Who's that? A sibling I don't know about?"

"Oh, come on, Sammy. You always get good grades. You've been on honor roll since you were, like, in nursery school."

"Nursery school? *Puh-leeze.* I was on honor roll in the *womb*, bro."

"Yeah . . . and I'm the loser."

He's not joking anymore. He's serious.

"RJ, you are so *not* the loser," I tell him. "Mom and Dad worship the ground you walk on."

He rolls his eyes. "No, that's you, Sammy. Me? I'm the one they worry there's something wrong with because I don't get good grades."

How is it that I've lived in the same house with my brother for all these years, sleeping in the room next door, but I never realized that he felt this way? I want to hug him, but I'm pretty sure it would freak him out.

I give his shoulder a gentle pat instead.

"There's nothing wrong with you, RJ," I tell him. And then, deciding that things are getting a little too mushy, I add, "Well, except for the fact that you're my little brother and a total pain in the butt."

"There'd be something wrong with me if I *wasn't* a pain in your butt," he says. "It's in my job description."

"Maybe you have a point," I admit.

We sit in a rare, companionable silence for a few minutes, taking turns stroking Scruffles' silky ears.

"So don't you think it's unfair?" RJ says. "Mom and Dad punishing you for something they found out by reading the stuff they made us promise not to read?"

"Yeah," I tell him. "It's pretty hypocritical."

"Totally hypocritical," he agrees.

But you lied. You went to the concert. You borrowed Mom's sweater without asking and shrank it.

Is this what feeling remorse is about? Guilt creeping up and surprising you when you least expect it, and making you realize that you're kind of responsible for what happened in the first place, even if your parents did say one thing, then do another?

"I . . . Well, even though it's hypocritical, the fact is, I *did* lie to them," I admit. "I went to the concert when they said I couldn't."

"I guess," RJ says. "Okay, so you did something wrong. But they're wrong, too—and aren't *they* the ones who always say, 'Two wrongs don't make a right'?"

When did my little brother get to be so smart?

"You know something, RJ? I've been underestimating you," I admit.

"You're not alone." He sighs. "Pretty much everyone does."

"Mom and Dad don't," I tell him.

"Trust me, they do," he says, giving Scruffles one last scratch behind the ears and getting up from the bed. "I should know."

He heads to the door and stops when he gets there. "Good luck when Dad comes home."

"Thanks," I say. "Although right now, being yelled at by Dad is the *least* of my worries." Then I throw myself back on my bed and bury my face in Scruffles' neck.

I know Dad's home because (a) I hear the garage door and (b) Scruffles leaps off my bed with a whine of excitement and runs downstairs, tail wagging, to greet the guy who brings home the bacon—or in the dog's case, the Beggin' Strips. I'm like a condemned prisoner in my cell, waiting to hear his footsteps on the stairs so I can get my *You are such a disappointment of a daughter* lecture over with. Ten minutes pass. Then twenty. I try to be productive and study, but it's hard to focus with the sword of Damocles hanging over your head. Maybe he's dragging this out just to torture me.

But then I realize he's probably showing the cyber-security guy who's going to look at our home network what's what. I hope this means I'll get my phone back and be able to use my laptop again. I have to know what is going on.

Or do I?

When Dad finally knocks on the doorframe and comes into my room, it's almost a relief because at least I don't have to anticipate the sermon anymore. My dad is here and ready to berate. He's also carrying my cell phone, which means I must be getting it back.

"I can't tell you how disappointed we are in you, Samantha," he says, going for the knife in the heart straight away. "We've always trusted you implicitly, Mom and me. To find that you so blatantly abused our trust like this . . ."

Dad shakes his head, looking at me sadly. "It almost makes me feel like I don't know you anymore."

He achieves his goal, which is to make me feel even more awful than I do. I have to hand it to Dad; he's a master at laying on the guilt. But in the back of my mind, a quiet voice speaks. It says: *"Hypocrite."*

It's that voice that gives me the courage to go straight back on the attack instead of taking my lecture meekly.

I steel myself and say, "You know what, Dad? After reading some of the stuff you wrote in those emails, I feel like I don't know *you* anymore, either. I can't believe my own dad makes racist jokes and tolerates sexism."

The seconds that follow are surreal; it's as if time has slowed, because every small movement of Dad's face is magnified. The widening, then narrowing, of his eyes, the dropping of his lower lip, then the tightening of his mouth into a thin, angry line, the exhale, then sudden inhale of breath.

"I told you not to read those emails," he says, shooting words out like bullets. "You promised you wouldn't. Was that just another lie?"

My most private thoughts are posted on the Internet and my parents have grounded me till after the SAT because they read them after making *me* promise not to read anything of theirs that the hackers posted. And now Dad's accusing me of lying because I read something that was on the front page of every single paper? The slowly simmering fury of the quiet voice inside finally boils over.

"Are you *serious*?" I explode. "I didn't lie. In case you missed it, that news was on the front page of all the papers. As Mom would say, it made *pretty eye-opening reading*."

Dad's face pales as he realizes his mistake, and he opens his mouth to speak, but he doesn't get a chance because I'm on a roll.

"I'm sick of this! I've spent sixteen years doing everything right and I do *one thing* wrong and it's the end of the world. But meanwhile, because of what *you've* done, my whole life is ruined."

"Stop exaggerating, Sammy. Yes, it's going to be difficult for a while, but your whole life isn't ruined."

"Isn't it? So when college admission officers google me and find my freaking journal online, that's not going to hurt my chances of getting in? Or what about when I apply for a job? Are you telling me that bosses aren't going to google me, either?"

That gives Dad pause, because he knows I'm right on both counts. My parents are the ones who are always warning me about posting stupid or inappropriate things online for that very reason.

He exhales slowly. "Look, I'm not going to pretend this hasn't caused our family damage and life going forward will be easy," Dad says. "Do you think it's been a cakewalk going to work every day?"

"No," I admit. I've noticed more fine lines around Dad's eyes and streaks of gray in his hair. Even now, there's a slight tremor in his fingers that I never noticed before. But then again, he's in charge, so wasn't it his job to make sure this didn't happen in the first place?

Is our family going to survive this?

"I know I haven't been the best father lately, and I'm sorry. But Winston Churchill said 'never to surrender ourselves to servitude and shame, whatever the cost and the agony may be,'" Dad reminds me. "It's going to be agony for a while. Trust me, I'm not underestimating the cost to you and RJ. I worry about you guys constantly." He gives me a brief hug. "But Mom and I need to be able to trust you to do the right thing. Especially now, with so much else going on. Okay?"

"Okay," I mumble, not really sure how we got from my dad's emails to inspiring Winston Churchill quotes. But it's not okay. Because he hasn't explained the stuff I read in his emails. He's just sort of stepped around it and that makes me feel worse. I wanted there to be a good reason for my dad saying such terrible things. There has to be more to the story than what was in the email. But if there is, he isn't telling me. And that just makes me wonder if maybe there isn't—if some things are just black and white.

And what I wonder, but don't have the courage to say, is if I can trust *him* to do the right thing anymore.

"Here's your phone," he says, handing it to me.

"What about my laptop?" I ask.

"You'll get it back later tonight, as soon as the cyber-security expert assures me that our home situation is secure."

He turns to leave, his shoulders hunched as if burdened by heavy weight.

"Dad?"

"Yes, Sammy?"

I can't help myself and the words rush out: "Mom said I'm grounded till after the SAT and I can't go out to anything. Even prom." I look at him pleadingly. "But . . . it's *prom*, Dad."

My dad frowns. "When you make a bad decision, you have to learn to live with the consequences," he says.

"But, Dad . . ." My fists clench in frustration as I bury my face in my hands. I know I brought the punishment on myself, but because of the hack, it feels like I'm being punished out of all proportion.

I sense him walking toward me and feel his hand on my shoulder. I pull away as I look up, feeling my teeth grinding together as I wait for him to speak.

"Here's the deal," he says, his hand dropping to his side.

"You can earn back the right to go to prom. I'm not making any promises. But if you behave well between now and then, you can go."

"Thanks, Dad. I'll be good. I promise."

What I don't tell him is that I don't even have a date yet.

April 10

My parents actually expect me to go to school today. But I don't think there's a strong enough outer shell in the universe to protect me now that the hackers posted my journal. It's like being the emperor who wears no clothes, except it's my bare naked thoughts being paraded around Brooklawne High. And it's not just around my school. Around the whole freaking world.

There's no way I can walk into that building. Not with all those eyes staring at me, all the whispering mouths.

Last night I made the mistake of going on Instagram. Someone took a screenshot of my probability trees of Jamie asking me to the prom and tagged both Jamie and me. So there's a ZERO percent probability that he hasn't seen it. I made my Instagram private, but even still—the comments people made, people who don't even know me (and even some who do), made me cry myself to sleep. They've been playing over and over in my head like one of those marquee signs in Times Square, ever since I woke up.

If it wasn't for Scruffles curled up next to me on the bed, I think I'd totally lose it. The soft inhale and exhale of his breath and the warmth of his furry body remind me that there's at least one living being on this planet who still loves me and thinks I'm wonderful.

Last night I promised Dad I would do the right thing so I could earn back the right to go to prom. But doing the right thing is going to have to start tomorrow, because there's no way I'm going to school today. Not on your life.

NINE

Mom wants to drive me to school, but I tell her I'm going to take the bus. RJ looks at me like I'm insane for wanting to do that, today of all days, but what he doesn't know is that I don't plan to take the bus at all.

"Are you sure, Sammy?" Mom asks. "Today's going to be tough."

"Tell me something I don't know," I say.

"It's not going to be an easy day for *any* of us," she says. "So maybe you could put the snark on hold?"

I didn't even think I was *being* snarky. I thought I was just being me. "Sorry," I mumble. "But it's fine. I'll take the bus."

Picking up my backpack, I head for the door. "Hey, RJ," I call over my shoulder. "Don't let the dimwits get you down."

"I'll try," he says through a mouthful of cornflakes, which is totally gross, but I give him a pass because his day is going to suck enough as it is.

Scruffles follows me out the door and as far as he can down the driveway before the electric fence warning kicks in. I give him a good-bye pat and keep walking. When I look back, he's still there waiting, watching me, his fluffy tail firmly hidden.

I wish I could tell him that I'll be back sooner than he thinks.

There's an old cemetery about a half mile from our house—and when I say old, I mean so old that nobody's been buried there for well over a century. A bunch of gravestones stick out of the ground like jagged teeth within a crumbling stone wall that you enter through a surprisingly ornate iron gate. Most of the gravestones are so worn you can't even read them. And while it's kind of creepy to be here by myself, I figure it's probably the best place to hide out until Mom leaves with RJ.

The gate creaks loudly as I push it open. It hasn't been oiled or painted in years, and the New England winters have taken a toll; rust clings to it like barnacles on the bottom of a boat.

It's just me and the old New England dead people, chilling until Mom takes RJ to school in . . . I check my phone—thirty-five minutes. By that time I'll be more than chilling. I'll be freezing. I should have worn a warmer jacket. The sun made it look warm in my bedroom, but here in Graveyard Central not so much.

Wait. Isn't spirit activity preceded by a blast of cold air?

I look around nervously, half expecting to see a ghostly colonial dude in a tricorn hat. Maybe . . . what's the barely legible name on this gravestone here . . . Obadiah Prescott. Nope. It's just a chill spring breeze. Obi-P Kenobi had a wife, Constance, and four kids, who are all buried here, too. One of his kids didn't even make it to a year old, poor little thing.

Things were tough in those days. At least Prudence Prescott, died age seventeen, didn't have to worry about the content of her brain being posted for the entire world to see. But with a name like Prudence, she was probably too smart to write down the contents of her brain in the first place.

My feet are cold. And my fingers are cold. I curl them around my cell, tempted to see what's happening online.

"What would you do, Prudie?" I ask the gravestone.

Dead leaves scrape across the stone as the wind blows them over to the next grave. Kind of like how my thoughts are being carried from one place to the next, except it's not by the wind, it's over the Internet.

After last night, I decided to stay off social media and stick to news. There's enough danger in the facts, without diving into everyone's opinions.

The *New York Times* reports that Aisha Rana, the executive in the New Territories Bank emails, is suing for discrimination in both state and federal courts on the basis that the company knowingly conspired to pay her less for the same job than they would pay a man. The lawyer for the bank claims that the emails can't be admitted as evidence because they weren't legally obtained.

That just sounds like they're weaseling so they don't have to admit they did something wrong, if you ask me. It's all kinds of messed up. Dad's the CEO of the bank. He shouldn't have let her be paid less in the first place, and once he did, he should be honest and face the consequences, the same way he and Mom expect me to do about going to the concert.

Too bad I can't ground my parents.

I check the time—another twenty-five minutes till I can go back to the house—and put my phone back in my pocket. The news is just driving me nuts.

Instead, I take out *The Light Between Oceans* and find a rock to sit on—making extra sure it's not a gravestone first because the last thing I need right now is to rile up some seventeenth-century spirit.

I read a few chapters, when I come to this: "We live with the decisions we make, Bill. That's what bravery is. Standing by the consequences of your mistakes."

The wind picks up and the gate creaks and slams closed against the latch. F-R-E-A-K-Y. The goose bumps that rise on my skin aren't because of the cold.

If standing by the consequences of your mistakes is bravery, I guess sitting here reading this book in a graveyard while pretending to my parents I'm at school must mean I'm a coward. And now I'm freaking out that a seventeenth-century ghost has come to tell me just exactly how much of a coward I am.

I shudder and snap the book shut.

Fortunately, when I check my phone this time, it's late enough that Mom and RJ should have left.

Stiff from the cold, I stand and brush the dead leaves and dirt off my jeans. I pause before Prudence Prescott's grave and quickly say the Shema. I know it's not the right prayer and she wasn't even Jewish, but I want to show respect, and it's the thought that counts, right?

Then, pulling my coat tighter around me, I head for home.

Scruffles greets me as if I've been gone for a week instead of like an hour. He barks and jumps up to lick my face.

"Okay, okay, crazy dog," I tell him. "I missed you, too. Now relax and let me take off my coat!"

It's strange to be home by myself at this time of the morning when I'm not sick. Until two days ago, I'd never skipped a single class, ever. Now I'm turning into a Grade A truant. See what these hackers have done to me? And what did I ever do to them? Nothing, that's what—other than being born Dick Wallach's daughter.

It's so unfair. But as I'm learning more and more every day, life isn't fair. What I have to figure out now is how to live with knowing that.

Taking my phone out of my coat pocket, I text Rosa.

**hey. ditching school today because of diary dump. i'm
sorry about it all. was supposed to be private.**

I wait to see if she texts back. Nothing. Maybe she's in the
part of B wing where there's lousy Wi-Fi signal. Or maybe
she's in class and can't text without it being obvious.

Or maybe she's so angry about what she read that she's not
talking to me.

I try Margo:

**hi. cutting school today because i can't face everyone.
even you and rosa. i'm sorry about the stuff in my diary.
never thought anyone would read it. is it terrible at
school?**

Nothing from Margo, either.

Maybe they both have broken cell phones.

Or maybe both Margo's and Rosa's parents forgot to pay
their cell phone bills?

Yeah, right.

More like they probably both aren't talking to me. Things
just keep getting more awesome.

I slump onto the sofa, pick up the remote, and turn on the
TV. Scruffles jumps and curls up beside me, his presence a
warm comfort.

Channel after channel of boring nothingness. Talk shows.
Toddler shows. News channels. Definitely skip. I can't even
find a decent cartoon or movie I want, to take my mind off
everything that's going on outside this house. Sighing, I drag

out *The Light Between Oceans* from my backpack. Might as well use the opportunity to finish it.

A few days ago, I couldn't imagine living on that remote island with no Internet. Today it seems like a much more attractive proposition.

The phone rings. I see from the caller ID that it's Mom, so I ignore it. Then my cell rings. That's Mom, too. I press IGNORE.

Then she texts.

WHERE ARE YOU?!!! I'm getting unexcused absence emails left, right, and center.

CALL ME IMMEDIATELY. :/

"I guess I better call her," I tell Scruffles. "Even though it's the last thing in the world I want to do—well, except for going to school."

Mom picks up on the first ring.

"Samantha Wallach, where are you?" she yells. "I've been worried sick. And I've got enough to worry about right now."

"I'm at home," I tell her.

"Why aren't you at school?" Mom asks in the cold, steady voice that means she's beyond livid. "And why didn't you pick up the phone?"

"I didn't pick up the phone because I didn't want you to know I wasn't at school," I say. "And I'm not at school because . . . because I couldn't face it, Mom. You read my journal. You saw what was in there. How am I supposed to go to school and face people ever again?"

Silence, except for Mom's breathing, which sounds a little ragged.

"Sammy, you can't cut the rest of junior year. You're going to have to face people."

"I know, Mom. But . . . I just couldn't face doing it *today*. I was up at four in the morning stressing about it."

"Everything looks worse at four in the morning, Sammy. It's the most lonely, miserable time," Mom says, her voice gentler now. "I'll call school and explain what's going on. They'll probably still count this as an unexcused absence, but at least they'll know there are extenuating circumstances. But, Sammy—"

"Yes, Mom?"

"Next time, ask. Don't just cut school and scare the heck out of me when I get the email and don't know where you are."

"What? Are you serious? You mean, come to you and say, 'Hey Mom, I want to skip school today'? Like you'd ever in a million years say yes?"

"Not if you just said, 'I want to skip school,' but if you explained how you were feeling like you did just now, then maybe we could decide you need a mental health day."

I can't believe my mom is being so . . . reasonable. I feel like asking her who she is and what she's done with my mom, but she asked me to hold the snark this morning.

"Thanks, Mom," I say instead. "That's what I'll do next time."

"At the rate you've been skipping school, there better not be a next time for a while," Mom warns. "I'll see you later. Love you."

"Love you, too," I mumble, and hang up.

Since I'm now home on a parentally sanctioned mental health day, I figure I might as well make cookies. This has the dual benefit of thanking Mom for being so understanding and allowing me to pig out on cookie dough, the perfect food for my current mental state.

When the third tray of cookies is in the oven, I get a text from Noah.

where are you today? you okay? BTW, i finished the light between oceans. wow.

home. mental health day. making cookies. yeah, i know, wow.

cookies? :) save me one!

what's the magic word?

abracadabra? oh, wait, PLEASE! :p

okay, will do.

srsly, are you okay?

My thumbs pause over the keypad. How do I answer that question? Do I lie and say, "Yeah, fine?" like people expect? Or should I risk being honest?

not so great. rosa and margo aren't returning my texts. the thought of going to school tomorrow makes me sick.

hang in there. but if necessary, alfred pennyworth will be there with a barf bag for you.

Despite my dread of going to school tomorrow, I laugh.

thanks. i hope i don't need it.

I just have to keep remembering that Winston Churchill quote Dad keeps repeating: "Never give in. Never give in. Never, never, never . . ."

Easy for old Winnie to say. He had a security detail.

In high school, you're on your own.

Except at least I know I'm not 100 percent on my own. And that makes it a tiny bit easier. Assuming that Noah doesn't read my journal and change his mind, that is.

April 10

Got a long lecture from Dad when he got home about "facing up to my problems rather than avoiding them" and "not being a quitter" and "Do you really want to earn back the right to go to prom, because if so, you've got a terrible way of showing it . . ."

When he said the part about facing up to problems rather than avoiding them, I was soooooooooooo tempted to say, "What, you mean like how you're facing up to the problems of not paying your female executives as much as the men?" but since Jamie Moss is asking someone to prom tomorrow and that someone still could be me, zipping it was probably the smarter move.

But it's painful to have to swallow all that anger. Sometimes I feel like I'm choking on it. And I mean seriously—talk about being a hypocrite! Dick Wallach, the CEO who is on the front page of every single freaking newspaper and business magazine in the country for not holding himself or his subordinates accountable (the same publications that previously praised him for his exceptional leadership skills) is lecturing me about personal responsibility? As Grandma Sally would say, "That takes chutzpah!" He's the new poster guy for failing to do what it took to protect the bank's customers from cyber attack. Forget the customers. He didn't protect me from it, either. I practically have to bite through my tongue to stay silent.

After I made the cookies, I packed some up to take to Noah, and some for Rosa and Margo as peace offerings. Then I chilled with Scruffles and finished <u>The Light Between Oceans</u>. It was a three-tissue ending. Scruffles commando-crawled over and put his head on my knee, because he was worried about me crying.

"It's okay, Scruffs," I told him. "It's just a book."

I don't know why I felt the need to lie to my dog.

Because the line that set me off was this: "Perhaps when it comes to it, no one is just the worst thing they ever did."

It made me think about Dad. It made me think about me, and how I'm afraid my best friends hate me. Neither of them have responded to my texts.

I want them to give me a break, to remember that our friendship is more than just the stupid rants I wrote in a journal I thought no one would ever see. But does that mean I have to figure out how to give Dad one, too?

TEN

Dad drops me off at school on the way to work. "Keep your chin up, Sammy," he says. "Remember: Never surrender to servitude and shame—"

"Yeah, I know. Churchill," I say as I get out of the car. "And thanks to events that have nothing to do with me, there's a greater than fifty percent chance this day will be filled with agony."

I slam the car door on whatever Dad planned to reply and start stomping toward the front entrance of school before I remember that I should keep up the front of *meh*. Complete nonchalance.

Stop. Deep breaths. Activate zombie self.

Especially because today's the day. The day I put off by skipping—when I have to face judgment at school. I'm shaking, and want nothing more than to go home, close the curtains, crawl under the covers, and hide with Scruffles curled up on the bed next to me.

But I can't do that forever, as much as it seems like the best plan right now, because whether I like it or not, life goes on. And I have to go on with it, no matter how awful it will be.

On the other hand, there's this: I know from my Secret Spying that today is also Jamie Moss promposal day.

The rest of my life leaves plenty to be desired, what with the hack and being grounded and wondering if my dad is really who I always thought he was. But today, Jamie Moss is going to ask someone to the prom, and until he's asked, that someone can still be me. It's like Schrödinger's cat, but with the prom, if the box is the promposal, and I'm the cat. Or wait, am I the cat or the person who opens the box? Maybe the ask is the cat and I'm the person who opens the box, so until I open the box, he could either have asked me, or someone else.

It makes me wish I could freeze this moment, because the box is unopened and so there's still hope and possibility.

If Jamie does ask me, then I know I can work my way back to Most Well Behaved Daughter status and earn back the right to go to prom. I've been a good Hamster Girl for all my life until this month. I know what to do.

I try not to notice that kids are staring at me and whispering as I walk into school. I'm not sure I can do this. The entire school has probably read everything by now.

Why should I have to earn back the right to go to prom?

My parents should owe me for making me suffer this agony for something that has nothing to do with me. But maybe this is a sign that if I open the box and the cat is dead, I should be relieved rather than devastated. If Jamie doesn't ask me, then I won't have to go face all the stares.

The student center is even more crowded than usual. I spot Noah and think of the cookies for him in my backpack. Strangely I wish I could stand with him because it would feel safe. At least I know he doesn't entirely hate me. He cared enough to check in on me yesterday.

The problem is that it would be awkward to be with one guy when another guy asks you to the prom.

If that first guy asks you, that is.

I finally catch sight of Rosa on the far side of the student center. She's sitting with Eddy Lau and looking happy and animated. I think, despite all Rosa's protests about them just being friends, they're becoming a thing. I start to head in her direction, even though I don't know what her reaction will be, but I'm only halfway across the student center when the music starts. Everyone starts looking around to see who is behind what is obviously another promposal, but I already know. It's Jamie. The ask is happening.

My heartbeat quickens as Jamie bursts through the doors of the student center, holding a red rose, with Nick Snow capturing his every movement on video. I can barely breathe as he starts looking around.

I'm over here.

His eyes continue searching, rest on me for a brief instant, and move on.

Probability zero.

The box is open and Schrödinger's cat is dead as a doornail. I don't feel relief. I'm paralyzed watching Jamie Moss go up to Geneva Grady and hand her the rose as Peter O'Doule and Daryl Williams unroll a sheet that says *PROM?* in big letters, and Jason Fremont opens a bag of gold and silver helium balloons, which float up to the ceiling.

Say no, Geneva. Say no.

But she doesn't. She nods and smiles. The sound of everyone in the student center clapping and cheering for my crushed dream unfreezes me. Luckily, the attention is on them as I move to the doors and run as fast as I can to the nearest bathroom, where I lock myself in a stall and bite my lip so I won't cry. But it doesn't work.

I have nothing to look forward to anymore. Nothing at all.

Except taking four APs and the SAT and being grounded until all the tests are over. Joy.

I never understood the importance of being able to believe in the possibility of a live cat inside that stupid box. Until this exact moment, when I'm sitting on a toilet in the school bathroom, hiding from the world. Without it, life seems like a bleak expanse of nothingness.

The bathroom door opens and two girls come in, talking excitedly about Jamie's promposal. Just my luck, it's two of Geneva's friends, Tanika Ward and Mackenzie Kilkenny. Great. The bell is going to ring in three minutes and I have to wash my face, which means I can't stay in this stall till they've gone or I'm going to be late for class. They're definitely going to see that I've been in here crying.

Could my life get any worse?

At least there's still toilet paper in this stall. You can't always count on that these days. I blot my eyes and then use the cover of flushing the toilet to blow my nose. Hoping it's not totally obvious that I've been losing it, I open the door and force myself to go out and face them.

Tanika's in a stall, but Mackenzie's at the sink putting on lip gloss. She gives me a dirty look at first, until she really sees my face in the mirror. "Oh . . . Sammy. Are you okay?"

"Yeah. I'm fine," I lie.

"It's just . . . you look like you've been crying."

"No, I'm fine. Really."

The big sniff following that statement probably diminishes my credibility, but what can I do? My nose isn't cooperating with the attempt at subterfuge.

I wash my hands, avoiding Mackenzie's gaze, pretending I really went to the bathroom and wasn't just crying my eyes out in the stall because Jamie Moss asking Geneva Grady to the prom instead of me was the final nail in the coffin of my doomed social life.

When I look up, her eyes meet mine in the mirror, filled with pity and something I can't figure out. It makes me want to slide down the drain with the soap bubbles. It's bad enough suffering total public humiliation, without having to face the pity.

"Look, Sammy, you said some nasty stuff about Geneva in your diary, and she's my friend and I'm mad at you for that, but . . ."

"I'm sorry," I say. "That was supposed to be private. I never thought anyone would see it."

"That doesn't make it any less mean," Tanika calls from the stall before she flushes.

I wait till she comes out before replying.

"I know," I say. "But . . ." I swallow, trying to find the courage to ask. "Can you honestly tell me you've never said anything mean about anyone? Ever?"

Mackenzie and Tanika exchange a glance, which tells me if they say they haven't, they'll be lying.

"I can't," Tanika admits. "I was trash-talking you something awful when I read what you wrote about Geneva."

"Me too," Mackenzie said. "But then . . . well . . ."

I get this feeling, suddenly, that there's something I'm missing here.

"We're really sorry about your mom," Tanika says, her brown eyes filled with genuine compassion.

My mom? What is she talking about?

"I'm praying for her," Mackenzie said.

"Yeah, me too," Tanika says. "My mom sent an email to our church prayer circle so everyone's been offering up prayers."

Prayer circle? They make it sound like my mom is at death's door or something.

My parents told me not to read the hacked stuff that was published online. Dad said it was "private, personal information, obtained illegally."

Apparently no one else got the memo.

Which means they know something that I don't.

"Um, why are you praying for my mom?"

Tanika gasps, and she covers her mouth with her hand. Mackenzie stares at me, horrified.

"You d-don't . . . *know*?" she stammers.

"Know what?" I persist.

The bell rings. Great, we're all late for class now, and I still don't know what it is that I don't know.

"We gotta go," Tanika says. "You should ask your parents."

She grabs Mackenzie, who is nodding her agreement like a crazed bobblehead, and drags her out of the bathroom as fast as they both can without running.

Saved by the bell. Which doesn't help me.

I take out my phone and text my parents.

what's going on? why are people holding prayer circles for mom? what aren't you telling me?

It's only a few seconds before my mom replies.

Go straight to the office. I'm coming to pick you up from school.

My breakfast flips over in my stomach and I have to swallow, hard, to keep it down. If Mom is coming to take me out of school, that means . . .

That means that whatever it is that Tanika and Mackenzie are talking about must be true.

When I get to the office and say my mom's coming to pick me up, Mrs. Vaner, whose nickname is the Dragon Lady—and not just because of her long red nails—tells me in a soft calming voice I never imagined could come out of her mouth, "Your mother already called us, Sammy dear. Have a seat. She said she'd be here in fifteen minutes."

More frightened than ever by her uncharacteristic niceness, I sink into the nearest chair, wondering what is going on.

"Do you want a cupcake?" Mrs. Vaner asks me. "I made them for Mrs. Bell's birthday."

"No, thanks," I say, because the Dragon Lady being nice to me makes me lose whatever appetite I might have for comfort food. It's a sign that something must be seriously wrong. Besides, I have a lifetime supply of undelivered cookies in my book bag.

Then the school psychologist, Mrs. Heller, comes out of her office. "Samantha," she says. "Why don't you come sit in here while you wait for your mother?"

Okay, whatever this mystery thing with Mom is must be something really, really bad. I wonder if my parents are getting divorced. Maybe the hackers released more New Territories stuff and Mom found out Dad was having an affair with someone from work or something. It's not anything I would have thought possible before, but after having read the sexist stuff he wrote in those emails, what do I know?

How do any of us really know everything about the people we love and think we know? Guess my mom was right when she said trust was hard to build and easy to lose. Not that I'll admit that to *her*.

I shuffle into Mrs. Heller's office and sit in the chair as far away from her desk as possible. It's not like I'm here for counseling or anything.

She shuts the door and sits in the other chair, instead of behind the desk. Leaning forward, she gives me a concerned look.

"Sammy. How are you holding up?" she asks. "I'm here whenever you need to talk."

"Uh, good to know," I say. "I'll keep it in mind."

Mom better get here soon. This is seriously awkward.

"How have things been? Are other students . . . making your life unpleasant?"

What does she think? That they're showering me with flower petals and telling me how awesome I am? I skipped school yesterday and didn't even make it to my first class today, but I'm already getting the cold shoulder from my best friends and people are staring at me like I'm a freak.

I stare down at my hands, unsure of how to answer.

"You had an unexcused absence yesterday," Mrs. Heller says. "Your mom called to explain about your need for a 'mental health day'"—she does air quotes while saying this—"but without a doctor's note, it still counts as unexcused."

So much for the parental pass. Chalk up two points in the Bad Girl Sammy column.

"I know this might be tough, but running away doesn't solve anything," Mrs. Heller continues.

I look up at her. "Easy for you to say."

"You're right. It *is* easy for me to say, when you're the one who has to live it. But I'm here to help you do it—and so is the rest of the team here at Brooklawne."

There's a "team"? Do they get letter jackets?

It's like having a conversation in a language I've only just started learning, because I guess I'm the only one who doesn't know the full extent of the "it" I'm supposed to be living through. People are praying in circles for my mother and I don't know why. How messed up is that?

"Yeah, thanks," I mumble, stealing a glance at the clock over her head. When is Mom going to get here?

"Things are hard now, but I'm sure everything will be okay," Mrs. Heller says in a comforting voice.

But I don't see how it can possibly be okay when I don't even know what's *not* okay.

Even though it makes me angry instead of comforting me, I can't say how I feel, because this is still school and the principal's office is only feet away.

When I finally see my mom walk into the office, I run out and launch myself at her, almost knocking her over with the force of my hug. I promptly burst into tears.

She winces. "Careful, Sammy," she says.

But I'm not in the mood to be careful. I just want to *know*. "Tell me," I sob into her neck. "What's going on?"

Mom pats my back, and I look up at her, noticing how she is uncomfortably aware of Mrs. Heller, Mrs. Vaner, and the rest of the office staff looking at us and listening. "Let's get out of here first," she says.

She signs me out, telling Mrs. Vaner that the principal authorized my release. After they exchange a knowing glance, we head to the parking lot. Things must be really, *really* bad.

"Mom, they said—"

"Sammy, please," Mom cuts me off before we even get to the front door. "I will tell you everything, but not until we're somewhere private. It's bad enough that our personal lives are being exposed like this—we don't have to add to the circus ourselves."

"I'm sorry if telling your own daughter things that everyone in the entire world seems to know is a circus."

My mom stops and turns to me. She cups my cheek with her hand and quietly, so softly I can barely hear her, she says, "I'm sorry."

I can't have heard her correctly. I think she said she was sorry.

My parents don't apologize. Not to us, anyway.

Before I can ask her to repeat what she just said, she turns and starts walking briskly toward the door, leaving me standing there, dumbfounded.

"Come on, Sammy," she calls back to me. "Let's go."

As I follow her to the door and out to the car, I watch for any clues of why she might be in need of Tanika's church prayer circle. Try as I might, I can't spot anything.

Except for the fact that she's come straight to school to pick me up, saying *we have to talk.*

The silence is thick between us as Mom pulls out of the school parking lot. I look at her out of the corner of my eye, waiting for her to start talking, to start telling me what is going on. She's biting the edge of her lip, the way she does when she's on the phone talking to Grandma Gertie, Dad's mom who lives in Florida, when Grandma's listing all the amazing and wonderful things her *other* grandchildren are doing (clearly implying that RJ and I are inadequate slackers).

We hit the first stoplight and Mom still hasn't said a word. I feel like I'm going to choke on my fear of unspoken words.

"Mom, *tell me*. What's the matter?"

She grips the steering wheel, hard. Blue veins in her hands are revealed like roads on a stress map. I wish she'd just say whatever it is. Or do I? Is this a cat box better left unopened?

"Let me pull over," she says, putting on her blinker. "I . . . It's better for me not to be driving."

I'm starting to think that maybe ignorance is bliss.

Mom manages to pull across two lanes of traffic and into the parking lot of the Orchard Street playground. She cracks the window slightly before she turns off the car, allowing in a sliver of fresh air and the sound of carefree toddlers playing.

Turning to me, Mom reaches over and takes my hand.

Now I'm really freaked out.

"Sammy, I should have told you this, *we* should have told you this before, but you have so much going on already with the SAT and APs coming up that Dad and I talked about it and we decided to wait," she says. "But then these hackers . . ."

She trails off, and I can't stand it for another second. I'm going to explode if I don't know what this is about. Right this very minute.

"Mom. *Please*. Just. Tell. Me."

My mother takes a deep breath and then exhales her news.

"Sammy, I have breast cancer."

Even though I've been expecting bad news, hearing the C-word come from Mom's mouth feels like driving into a wall of reinforced concrete at high speed. Everything shatters in an instant.

"Are you going to . . ."

I can't say *die*, because I'm afraid if I give name to my fear, it will happen.

My mother's eyes glisten with unshed tears.

"I certainly don't plan to *shuffle off this mortal coil* anytime soon," she says, mustering a smile. "I'm going to do everything I possibly can to avoid that possibility."

That's so Mom: telling me she's not going to die with a quote from the Great Bard.

But is she telling me the truth or just putting on a brave face so I don't freak out and bomb the APs? I mean, if Mom's been keeping something this important from me, how do I know I can trust her?

"It'll be okay," she says. "I'm going to the best doctors."

"But what did they say, exactly? Do you have to have chemo? Are you going to go bald?"

"I will have to have chemotherapy, yes. About three weeks after they operate," Mom says. "And yes, I'll lose my hair. They tell me that will probably start to happen a few weeks after the first round of chemo."

"Operate? When were you planning to tell us about that?"

Mom looks out the window. I follow her gaze to a little girl with brown hair in pigtails, tied with red bows that match her Wonder Woman T-shirt. Her short legs climb the ladder to the top of the slide with strength and confidence, and she slides down, hands in the air, laughing.

I wish I could trade places with her. She seems to have her life so much more together than I do.

"Dad and I thought . . ." Mom turns to look at me. "We thought it would be best to wait till after APs."

Well, at least now I know how long they were planning to lie to me. "When's the operation?"

My mom hesitates.

"*When*, Mom?"

"I go into the hospital for prep the afternoon of your last AP exam. They'll operate the following morning."

This is a horror movie wrapped in a nightmare I can't wake up from because I'm not sleeping.

"You were planning to tell me when I finished APs? *The day you were going into the hospital?*"

I'm shaking with a whirlwind of feelings I can't even begin to name. I can't believe my parents, who, they are constantly reminding me, are the wise, mature ones, actually thought this was a good idea.

"We didn't want to worry you when you already had so much on your plate," Mom said. "We know how important the AP exams are to your future."

"What, you mean as important as not having a mom?" My voice starts to break on the last word, giving me away.

Mom hugs me then, tightly, even though my shoulders are still stiff with anger.

"I'm going to fight this, Sammy," she says. "I promise, sweetheart, I'm going to fight it with everything I've got so I *am* here for you and RJ and Dad."

I give in to the comfort of her hug, and the tears, which I've been trying hard not to shed, make a wet patch on her linen shirt. Ugh. I've cried more this week than I have in all of high school. I wonder if it's scientifically possible for tear ducts to dry up from overuse?

"I don't want to put any more pressure on you than you've already got," Mom says. "But I'm going to need your help. I'm going to need everyone's help."

The familiar weight of anxiety slides down my forehead to rest between my eyebrows. My temples start throbbing.

"What can I do? I'm not a doctor."

"When you pass your driving test, you can help with grocery shopping and picking up RJ. I've got some friends who are going to help make meals, but you can help by making sure they get heated up and the dishes get done."

Just when I thought life couldn't get worse, now I get to be Cinderella, too. Except this Cinderella doesn't even get to go to the prom because her handsome prince just asked Geneva Grady.

I sigh and nod, saying, "Okay."

"I'll do my best to make sure it doesn't all fall on your shoulders, Sammy. I know this has been a shock, and I'm sorry you had to find out this way," she tells me.

"Me too," I mumble. "I felt so stupid. Random kids at school know my mom has cancer, but I don't? They must think I'm the World's Worst Daughter."

"You definitely aren't that!" Mom smiles. "Grandma Sally is going to help out, and I'm sure she'll assure you that *I* gave you a run for the World's Worst Daughter when I was your age." She pats my knee. "But I turned out okay in the end, and you will, too. Everything's going to be fine. We just have to think positively."

Like that's going to be so easy with my entire life going viral, all these Very Important Tests coming up, no date in sight for the prom, which I have no incentive to work to go to anyway, and now a mother with breast cancer. I can't exactly see the "half-full" part of the glass right now. Unless my glass is supposed to be full of Evil-Tasting Misery Slime, in which case it's about to overflow.

But I can't say that to my mom, who is trying to be upbeat about her cancer prospects for my sake, can I?

"Yeah. It's all good, Mom."

"Since I've signed you out from school, why don't we go get our nails done and have lunch?" Mom says.

I think of the AP prep I'm missing and which I'll now have

to catch up on during an open or after school tomorrow. Plus, what I missed yesterday and the day before. But looking on the bright side, I get another reprieve from having to face the consequences of the contents of my brain going viral.

"Sounds like a plan," I say, working my best *positive attitude* smile.

If I've learned one thing from this conversation, it's that my mom and I are terrible at lying to each other, but great at ignoring the fact that we're both doing it.

April 11

I spent most of today playing hooky from school with Mom. But even while I was worrying about her and promising myself that I would be nicer, I was super pissed about my parents' hypocrisy for reading my journal and punishing me for what they found, and then telling me I shouldn't read any of their stuff because it's private.

After this morning, all bets are off. Finding out that Mom has cancer from a girl in a bathroom at school instead of from my own parents? That's beyond messed up. If we're looking for silver linings here, it actually made me forget that I was upset about Jamie Moss asking Geneva Grady to prom instead of me, for a few hours. There will be other dances. I hope. If my life ever goes back offline. Anyway, I only have one mom. How is that for trying to think positively?

Okay, I'm working on it.

Mom said they were trying to "protect" me because I already have so much stress with APs and the SAT coming up, but you have to wonder what planet they were on when they thought that was a viable plan. Did they seriously think that with our private stuff plastered online and being reported in every freaking news outlet that no one at school was going to say anything? I hate to break it to you, dearest parents, but there's this newfangled thing called social media.

For smart people, my parents are great at being oblivious.

But who am I to talk, right? Wasn't I doing exactly the same thing with Jamie Moss? Is being oblivious inherited?

More importantly, is it curable? Because it sure seems like a stupid way to go through life.

Maybe the cure is having the courage to face the things that scare you. That's why I've decided to read what the hackers posted. If Mom and Dad can snoop into my private thoughts, it's only fair I get to look at theirs.

eleven

Dad actually comes home early from work, so he and Mom can sit RJ down for "the talk." Now that the cat is out of the bag, they can't put it off any longer.

I don't know how they thought they could keep that cat in the bag in the first place.

I'm in my room writing in my diary when my dad knocks and sticks his head around the door.

"Hey, honey. Mind if I come in?"

I pull the AP study guide over my journal so Dad can't see it. "No. I'm just here studying, as usual."

Dad comes in and sits on the end of the bed. "Don't worry, Sammy. Just a few more weeks and it'll all be over," he says.

I stare at him, wondering if either the stress has made him lose it or if he thinks I'm completely stupid.

"Really, Dad?" I ask, dripping snarkasm. "You think I'm dumb enough to believe this will all be over?"

Dad realizes his mistake and a wash of pink appears under his five o'clock stubble. "I meant *the AP exams*," he says.

"Sure, *they'll* be over. But which of the list of other things that *won't* be over do you want to cover first? The fact that you're a closet racist, that you allow sexism in the workplace, or that you and Mom thought it was a good idea *not* to tell us that she has cancer?"

For the first time in my life, I've shocked my dad into silence. I expected him to be mad, to shout back at me, but instead his shoulders sag.

"I'm sorry, Sammy. We made a mistake."

Guess we're only talking about the cancer here. One traumatic secret at a time . . .

He continues, "We were trying to do what we thought was best, and . . ." He sighs, heavily. "Looks like it didn't turn out that way, did it?"

They say you should count to ten before responding when you're really mad, but I can only make it to four before exploding.

"Seriously?" I ask. "How could you imagine for *one nanosecond* that someone wasn't going to blab to one of us about Mom having cancer?"

"That's what Grandma Sally said," Dad admits. "She told us we were crazy."

"Why didn't you listen?" I ask. "You always expect *us* to listen to *you*."

"Just like you listened when we told you not to go to that concert?" Dad retorts. "Or when Mom said not to borrow her clothes without asking her first."

Touché, Dick.

I avoid his gaze, and he knows he's got me. Sort of. I don't think sneaking out to go to a concert or borrowing clothes is exactly the same as keeping cancer a secret from your own kids. And he's conveniently avoiding talking about the work stuff. *Don't think this fact escapes me, Dear Old Dad.*

"Look, Sammy, we don't have all the answers," he says.

"You always act like you do."

"You want to know the truth?" Dad asks.

"No, *lie* to me," I say. "*Of course* I want to know the truth."

"Okay, but you have to promise not to tell RJ till he's older."

He leans in, and I'm wondering if he's going to reveal some deep dark family secret.

It's nowhere near that exciting.

"Most of the time we're faking it," Dad whispers.

"*That's* your excuse?"

"It's the truth, Sammy. No one hands you a How to Be a Perfect Parent manual when your kids are born," he says. "Your mom and I do the best we can, and sometimes we screw up because we're human, and as someone who reads as many books as you do knows, human beings are flawed. Even great parents like us."

Dad looks at me with a pointed smile. "And even great kids like you."

Okay. I'm a screwup. Whatever.

"But how could you have thought it was a good idea?" I persist. "I'd finally be breathing a sigh of relief that the APs were over and then you were going to hit me with 'Oh, BTdubs, Mom's got cancer and she's having an operation *today*!'"

My dad looks down at his hands, and I notice that the gray patches at his temples seem to have grown in the last week or so.

"Mea culpa," he says. "You can blame me for this more than Mom. I was so worried about you doing well on your exams that I didn't listen when wiser heads told me to look at the bigger picture."

"Yeah . . . like that Mom could . . ."

Dad sees the tears welling in my eyes, and he wraps me in a bear hug before I can say the word.

"Come on now, Sammy. We have to think positively," he whispers at my temple. "It's going to be okay. The prognosis is good, we're consulting with the top doctors, and Mom needs us to believe she's going to be fine. One hundred percent."

I rest my head on Dad's shoulder, willing myself to believe, and worrying about the consequences if I can't.

Dad pats my back and pulls away. "I've got to go talk to RJ. We haven't told him yet," he says. "But I wanted to talk to you first, to apologize . . . and to ask for your help. Because Mom and I are really going to need it."

"I know, I know. Making dinner, doing the dishes, all that fun stuff."

"And helping us to keep RJ in good spirits. It's going to be tough for all of us, especially with everything else that's going on." Dad drops a kiss on the top of my head when he gets up.

For a brief moment, in the warm comfort of my father's hug, I'd forgotten about the *everything else*. And honestly, right now, I don't have the energy to deal with it. So I let him get up to leave.

But of course it's all out there online, waiting. And anger and distrust is still bubbling within me like a slowly simmering volcano.

"Study hard," he says.

"I will," I promise. *Just not what you think I'm supposed to be studying.* "Can you shut the door, Dad? I need to concentrate."

"Sure thing," my dad says, closing the door behind him.

As soon as the latch clicks shut, I get my laptop and search for our name and hacked files. It takes all of three seconds to find a website that's posted all of them, and which has even conveniently broken them down into "texts and emails," "chats," and "S. Wallach journal."

Don't look at that, don't look at that, don't don't don't don't DON'T CLICK THERE!

The cursor hovers over the link to my journal. I didn't write those words expecting anyone to see them, and I know that there's a 100 percent probability that the comments are going to make me feel bad about myself and I shouldn't look at them if I want to keep a shred of my self-respect. So why is my finger itching to press on the link?

I guess it's the hope that even if there are two hundred people who make fun of me and say that I'm just a typical dumbheaded girl who only cares about some guy who will never ask her to prom in a million years, maybe there's someone, even if it's only one person, who read my words and understands. Who thinks, *Yeah, I've felt like that, too.*

Do I have the courage?

We've been reading T. S. Eliot's poem "The Love Song of J. Alfred Prufrock" in AP English Lit, which isn't much of a love song at all. I think it's more about not daring to live an authentic life because you're too afraid of what everyone else thinks. (Trust me, the irony hasn't been lost on this girl.)

To wonder, "Do I dare?" and "Do I dare?"

Time to turn back and descend the stair

No. I don't.

I'm just as much a wimp as J. Alfred Prufrock was when

T. S. Eliot wrote that poem over a hundred years ago. The world is more high-tech, but maybe people haven't changed much. We're still just as cowardly, and cruel. Technology just circulates what we say faster.

I decide to click on the emails instead. Since Mom and Dad read the texts between my friends and me, it's only fair that I get to read the stuff they sent to each other.

Here's a text exchange between Mom and Dad.

Mom: You better come home from work at a decent hour tonight or I might murder your daughter.

Murder his daughter? That's *me* she's talking about! Wow. Thanks a lot, Mommy Dearest. I love you, too.

Dad: Will do my best. Got enough headaches without having to bail you out of the slammer. :p

Ha-freaking-ha. Dad's not worried about Mom killing his only beloved daughter; he just doesn't want the headache of bailing his wife out of jail. My parents are a laugh riot.

Mom: I mean it, Dick. I'm not sure how much more of this fighting I can take. What happened to our daughter?

Dad: She's still there. Remember what your mother said.

Mom: I know, I know, "This, too, shall pass." But I might not live that long.

Gasping as I read those words, I check the date stamp on the email to see how long ago this exchange took place. March 28. Then I open the journal file on my laptop—the one that's now posted for the entire world to see.

March 28

I'm not sure how I can stand to live in the same house as my mother for another year and a half without either (a) committing matricide, or (b) my head exploding.

Nothing I do is right. I can't wait to go to college. Too bad I have to jump over so many insane hurdles in the next few months in order to get there. NO PRESSURE, RIGHT?!

I can't believe I talked about killing my own mom, even as a joke.

Did Mom know she had cancer then? So when she says, "But I might not live that long," is she joking or is it because my parents are lying to me about her prognosis?

Do they even realize that everything they say to me about trust is a two-way street? That I have to trust *them*, too?

Clicking on an email with the subject "RJ testing?" I read that Dad's written:

I'm worried about RJ's grades. I think we should have him tested. I think he has a learning disability of some kind that's preventing him from achieving the way he should. We need to make sure he has every support he needs to get into a top college.

I thought RJ was just being oversensitive. Turns out he was right.

Mom is a lot more laid-back when it comes to RJ than she is about me. No murderous impulses expressed about her beloved son.

There's nothing the matter with RJ. Maybe he's just not as academic as Sammy. He has other strengths.

Dad apparently didn't buy that argument.

You have a blind spot when it comes to him, Helene. You can't keep making excuses for RJ.

I hate that there are people outside our family reading this. I want to make RJ a fort of soft blankets and pillows like I did when we were little, so he can hide inside and none of this will hurt him.

If only it were that easy. I wouldn't mind living out the rest of high school in an awesome blanket fort.

Besides all her work stuff, there are emails about car pools, about who is picking up who when, about PTA meetings, book club meetings ("bring your fave dessert, a bottle of vino, and your opinion"), and other stuff that Mom has to deal with.

There's one with the subject line :(from Mom to Dad.

Sometimes I feel like Samantha hates me with every fiber of her being. Every single thing that comes out of my mouth is apparently evidence of what an out-of-touch, politically incorrect, wrong-about-everything person I am. After a particularly bad fight this morning, I found myself looking at pictures of toddler Sammy and me, longing for her to gaze at me with that look of love and reverence, as though I am the center of her world just for one day, instead of the usual scorn.

Yes, I know, I'm being pathetic and ridiculous. I keep telling myself what my mom and the parenting articles tell me: This is age appropriate. The teen years are when kids start to break away from their parents and form their own identities and ideas, and it's never an easy process—as Mom is always quick to remind me. But it's so exhausting. And incredibly painful.

Never mind me. I'm just having a bad morning. Scruffles is nagging me for walkies, and I'm sure we'll both feel better afterward.

XO Hels

Guilt blooms in my stomach. Because I don't hate my mom. I just wish she understood me a little more. Cut me some slack. Trusted me.

Dad wrote back to her:

Sammy loves you, Helene, even if she's not showing it right now. Give her time and space. You're a great mom and the love of my life. XO Dick.

I close the computer.

Gross. I feel like a voyeur reading my father's profession of love to my mother.

Except it's already been read 105,988 times, according to the website stats.

All those people know how much I've hurt my mom. My mom who has cancer.

They must hate me.

I can't really blame them.

I kind of hate myself right now.

Loud stomping comes up the stairs and then I hear RJ's door slam. For a few minutes, I debate if I should go to him, but I know that he must be freaking out after hearing about Mom. So I suck it up, go to his room, and listen outside the door. He's definitely crying, but the sound is muffled, like he's doing it into a pillow. I knock and say, "RJ, it's me," then go in without him saying it's okay, because whether he knows it or not, he needs me. Not just because of Mom. Because of what's happening outside our family.

The truth is, I need him, too.

My brother is curled up on his bed, with Scruffles lying next to him, licking the tears off his face. I sit on the bed and hug them both.

"What if Mom dies?" RJ sniffs.

I don't want to lie to him and say she won't, because I don't know if that's the truth, and I'm sick of lies. All I can tell him is what I *do* know.

"We're going to do everything we can to make sure that doesn't happen. All of us. You, me, Dad, the doctors, and most of all, Mom. Because that's the last thing that she wants" is what I say.

Scruffles gives me a lick as if encouraging me to go on.

"Mom wants to be here for us as much as we want her to be. She wants to see us graduate. She wants to see us get married and have kids."

"Ew. She's going to have to live a long time for the married part," RJ says. "Because I'm not getting hitched till I'm like . . . thirty. And kids . . . I don't know if I want them ever. Too much work."

I laugh. "Maybe if they're like *you*. I've been a total piece of cake to raise."

"Oh, right," RJ snorts. "Piece of cake, huh? Sneaking off to concerts and fighting with Mom all the time?"

That wipes the smile from my face. *You better come home from work at a decent hour tonight or I might murder your*

daughter . . . Sometimes I feel like Samantha hates me with
every fiber of her being.

"I guess I haven't exactly been all sugar and spice, huh?"

"Ya think? It's like living with a walking time bomb. We
never know when you're going to explode next."

It's not easy to look at yourself in the brother mirror, especially when you realize he's right. Taking a deep breath, I
tell him the conclusion I've drawn from reading the hacked
documents.

"Something's wrong with us, RJ, and it's not just Mom's
cancer."

"What do you mean?"

"Why didn't we know any of this before the hackers? How
come we never talked about it until now?"

RJ sits up suddenly, startling Scruffles, who circles and
then plops down again between us, gazing up at me with a
bemused expression.

"We do talk. At least we kind of talk. We have dinner
together more than a lot of my friends do. And we're not
allowed to have devices at the table like Tim's family or have
the TV on during meals, like Joe's," he adds. "When I go
to friends and they have a TV on during meals, they *really*
don't talk."

"Okay. So . . . we talk about getting good grades. About
getting into the best college so we can get a well-paying job.
About what movies we saw and where we're going on vacation,

and what happened at work," I point out. "But not about how I feel like I'm a hamster on a wheel that never stops and you feel like Mom and Dad think that there's something wrong with you and Dad says one thing at work and different things at home or that Mom has freaking cancer. That's what we don't talk about. Why did it take the hackers to show us what was happening in our own house?"

RJ fiddles with the tags on Scruffles' collar.

"Today this kid at school said, 'Your dad thinks you're a retard.' He said that it was in the emails the hackers posted."

I feel a flood of fury. I want to go to the middle school and punch this kid for saying that to my brother. What does he know?

Just what he read in Dad's email, I realize. My fury disappears.

"He's lying," I say, which is basically the truth. Dad didn't use the R-word. "Don't listen to him. Mom and Dad love you and they're proud of you."

"I wish we didn't have to go to school," RJ says. "I wish we could find some really rich person to lend us their luxury house on a private desert island where there's no Internet for a month or two, or however long it takes for this to blow over."

"I'd be up for that," I say. "It sounds like total heaven. As long as we go *after* my driving test."

April 12

It's three in the freaking morning and I'm wide-awake. You know things are bad when you're awake before the birds start singing the Dawn Chorus. I've tried getting back to sleep, but it's no good. I keep tossing and turning as I imagine how awful it's going to be walking into school today. At least yesterday the cat had the possibility of being alive in the box. But today the box is open, the cat is dead, my journal is public, my privacy is gone, and I still haven't heard back from my two best friends, even though I texted them about Mom's cancer.

There's a sharp pain in my stomach. I wonder if it's my appendix. On the plus side, having appendicitis would give me a good excuse not to go to school. But if I have appendicitis, I'd have to postpone my driving test, and that would be tragic. So I guess I'm going to have to suck it up. Find the courage to go to school and face all the people talking about me, judging me for the things I wrote in my journal. Find the courage to face the consequences of my actions—and the hackers' actions, too.

Today is the first full school day of the rest of my friendless, loser high school life.

It's going to be a wonderful day, I can tell already.

Oh, wait, I'm supposed to be thinking positively for Mom. I'm failing at that miserably, and it's only Day One. I've got to practice positive thinking so I get better at it. Nothing bad is going to happen to my mother because I'm being Ms. Glass

Half-Empty. No, I'm going to be a regular Annie from now on. "The sun will come out tomorrow!" "Tomorrow" is my new theme song, even though hearing it makes me want to poke out my eyeballs with a fork.

I'll go crazy in less than a day if I have that song as an earworm. An inspiring quote would be better. Winston Churchill must have said something. Sure enough, just searched for "Winston Churchill quotes, positive" and found this one, which is attributed to him but he might not have actually said. Whatever. It sounds like something he'd say.

"A pessimist sees the difficulty in every opportunity; an optimist sees the opportunity in every difficulty."

Okay, I have to start looking for the opportunities in my difficulties, which are currently . . . many. Let's see . . . Becoming a social outcast means I'll have more time to study for APs, and so I'll do really well and get into a top college and graduate and get a killer job. (And hopefully my boss won't make comments about me like Dad's colleagues did about Aisha Rana in that email.) Okay, that wasn't 100 percent positive. Baby steps.

Here's another maybe Churchillism:

"Success is not final, failure is not fatal: It is the courage to continue that counts."

As encouraging as it is to learn that failure isn't fatal, it's kind of a bummer to know that success isn't permanent. Does that mean the rest of my life is going to consist of more running on the same hamster wheel, just in a different place? Because, just, ugh.

No matter what the answer, it all comes down to finding the "courage to continue." Even if that means walking into school when you realize that most people have probably read your most intimate thoughts. If I can do it without wanting to hurl, I'll call that success.

Maybe I should listen to Grandpa Marty. He'll complain about his latest medical ailment—with Mom and Dad rolling their eyes in the background—but he inevitably finishes with a shrug and says, "Well, not to worry. It's better than the alternative."

When I was little, I never understood what the alternative was. It took me a long time to figure out he meant death.

Positive motto for today: "It's better than death."

At least I hope it will be.

TWELVE

Dad's already left for work by the time we get up for school, but Mom is armed with coffee, pancakes, and a pep talk.

"I know today is going to be hard," she says. "Not just today. It's going to be hard for a while."

"How long?" RJ asks. How can he still believe Mom knows all the answers?

"That's the tricky part," she says. "We don't know." She puts down her coffee mug and takes each of our hands. "But I am going to promise you this: We're going to get through this together, as a family."

I look her in the eye. "No more secrets?"

"No more secrets," she promises.

I really want to believe her.

Margo is standing out front with her student government friends when I get off the bus. She tries to give me the cold shoulder when I walk by, looking the other way and pretending she doesn't see me, but I'm not going to be an ostrich.

"Margo."

She turns and it's like looking into the face of a stranger. There's no warmth, no friendship. There's not even hot anger. There's just . . . cold indifference.

"What?" she says.

"I'm sorry," I say quietly. She's not going to make this easy for me.

"You should be," she says, and turns away.

I didn't expect her to forgive me right away, but I also didn't expect her to completely turn her back on me like this. Not when my mom has cancer.

"Maybe you should be, too," I say to her back. "It's not like you've been the best friend, either."

She whirls around and faces me. "What's that supposed to mean?"

"It means you didn't even call me when I texted you to tell you my mom has cancer. I don't care what happened between us. I would have called you."

"Sure you would," Margo sniffs.

I look her straight in the eye. "Yeah. I would have. And that's the difference between us."

I turn and walk away, biting my lip on the hurt and anger

that threatens to overflow. As I do, I can hear her bad-mouthing me to her friends. Which sucks. But, honestly, I kind of don't care at this point. I'll give her cookies to someone who deserves them more. Maybe I'll eat them myself.

I hope Rosa will be more understanding. We've been friends since first grade, which has to count for something. But she hasn't answered any of the texts I've sent her, even the one telling her about Mom's cancer. I thought she might call. Or at least send an emoji-filled text back. Something.

But instead . . . silence.

I can't stand the idea that I might lose Rosa.

I know I wrote some thoughtless things in my journal, but can they outweigh all our years of friendship? They weren't ever meant to be seen—they were just things I wrote to vent, in private. Can I really be blamed for this?

Jamie Moss is hanging out with his lax bro crew near the front door. If I had more time, I'd turn around and walk the entire way around the building to use one of the back doors to avoid having to pass by, but unfortunately, I don't have the option. I have to take a deep breath, activate my outer shell, and hope that Grandpa Marty is right and this really *is* better than the alternative.

"Hey, Sammy, what's the probability that you're the biggest nerd at Brooklawne High?" Nick Snow asks.

"Maybe we should make a decision tree to decide!" Peter O'Doule smirks.

Like you'd even know how.

"Nah, I think the probability is one hundred percent."

Even staring straight ahead, without looking, I know the last voice is Jamie.

Keep walking. Just keep going. Put one foot in front of the other and don't let them see you break.

"Did you see the pictures from her Photo Booth?" Nick sneers. "Nice duckface."

"More like dorkface." Jamie laughs.

He is such a tool. He's also stupid. He's the one who has been copying my freaking homework. That's what gives me the courage to turn around and say, "How would you know the first thing about probability, Jamie, when you copy my homework because you're too lazy and dumb to do your own?"

I don't stick around for a response. I'm more worried about making it into school without losing it. But the laughter follows me through the entrance and stays in my head after the door closes behind me.

How am I going to survive today? And even if I manage to get through today, how will I make it through the next day— and the day after that? Summer is still weeks away.

The weight of it all makes me want to curl up under a desk and hide.

Think positive. Look for the opportunities in your difficulties.

Drawing a blank here, Sir Winston. I'll have to get back to you on that later. If I live that long.

"Hey, Sammy—wait up!"

I turn around to see BethAnn Jackson hurrying to catch up with me. "Listen, Sammy, I just wanted to say . . . I read your journal and—"

She stops, seeing the stricken expression on my face. "Look, I'm sorry I read it, because I know it's private and I shouldn't have. But everyone else was reading it and they said you'd written about me, so . . ." She trails off, a slow flush tingeing her cheeks.

I stare at her, waiting.

"So anyway, I read it and I'm sorry . . . but I also wanted to say thank you," BethAnn finally says.

"For what?" I ask, surprised that anyone would be thanking me for anything today.

"For understanding. About how I felt when Gary Harvey asked me to the prom and everyone was chanting to say yes and so I did, but I didn't want to go with him, and then when I told him that after—"

"He made that awful video," I say.

She shudders. "I know! Like I owed it to him to go to prom because he'd already posted his promposal video on YouTube. I hate it. I don't even want to go to prom anymore."

"Well, I doubt I'll be going." I sigh. "Not now that everyone knows I make decision trees to calculate my preferences for the various outcomes of who might ask me."

BethAnn giggles. "You have to admit, it is pretty funny."

"According to Nick Snow, it makes me the biggest nerd at Brooklawne High."

"We all figure those odds vaguely in our head," BethAnn says. "You're just the only one I know who calculated it using actual numbers and probability trees. It's impressive in its own dorky way."

"Well, unfortunately, it means the probability of my having a date for the rest of my high school life is now zero," I say.

"Look, I know from what happened to me that it's not going to be a whole lot of fun for you at school for a while," BethAnn says. "And I just wanted to say . . . well, if you need someone to talk to, I'm here."

We've really only known each other superficially until now. But she's being nicer to me than my supposed best friends. I guess she knows how it feels to be ostracized for something that's out of your control.

"Thanks, BethAnn," I say. "That means more to me than you can imagine."

"Actually, I *can* imagine," she says with a grin. "You'll get through this. It's going to be brutal for a while, but don't worry. Sooner or later, the world will move on to the next thing."

"Roll on, next thing," I say. "I'm soooo ready for the world to move on."

It's kind of crazy-making when you walk into class and can't figure out if people are looking at you because they've read your innermost thoughts or if they just happen to be glancing in that direction or if they just hate your guts anyway or if maybe they just like the outfit you happen to have on that day. If I see two people whispering, I wonder if they've read my journal and they're saying I'm a nerd or I'm crazy or I'm awful for trash-talking other kids at school or criticizing my friends. Or maybe they're saying how messed up it is that I didn't even know my own mom had cancer until Tanika and Mackenzie told me in the girls' bathroom.

Or maybe they're not even talking about me at all and I'm just being paranoid, or thinking that I'm more important than I really am, because why would anyone care?

When I finally see Rosa, though, I know from the lack of greeting that she *has* read and she *does* care. She is so not happy.

"I've been texting you," I say, not really sure what else to say.

"I know," she responds.

I wait for her to tell me why she hasn't been texting me back, or she's sorry to hear about Mom's cancer, but . . . nothing. So I plow on. "I'm sorry about the stuff I wrote, Rosa. Really. I never thought anyone would see it."

"And that's supposed to make it better?" Rosa asks. "You

think it's okay to say stuff like that just because no one will see it?"

"No!" Well, maybe, I admit to myself. "But . . . c'mon, Rosa, are you telling me that every single thought you've had about me in the history of our friendship has been glitter and unicorns? That you've never ever thought or said a bad thing about me ever?"

"No, I'm not saying that, but—"

"All I did was write them down for me and someone else stole them and posted them online. It's not like I wanted the world to see those thoughts. If I wanted to hurt you, I would have said those things to your face. But they were just frustrations. You're my best friend. I would never go out of my way to be a jerk to you."

"And now everyone knows what you think of your supposedly best friends. If you talk like that about Margo and me when you like us, what kinds of things do you think and say about the people you *don't* like?"

"You know me. And you know what I say about people I don't like, because we've been talking about the same people for years."

"But I never thought you talked about *me*, Sammy. Not like that. Not the way you wrote in your journal."

"I don't *talk* about you like that. You just admitted you thought things. The only difference is that I wrote them down and got hacked," I point out.

But Rosa remains stony faced.

"Come on, Rosa. Things are beyond awful right now. I need my best friend."

"Maybe you should have thought of that before you wrote about how bad I smell and that *it's a cultural thing*," Rosa says before turning her back on me and walking away.

Oh. I forgot about that. Shame roils over me and I let her go. Because what can I say other than sorry?

It's impossible to find anything positive after I watch her back retreat down the hall. Other friends may have come and gone, but Rosa has been a constant, the North Star in my constellation of friendships. Do these people, these faceless hackers who've exposed my life to the world, do they have any idea how much harm they've caused, how many people they've hurt? My hands are clenched into tight fists as I walk to the media center, wishing I could use them on whoever decided it was okay to post my journal for everyone to read. What did I ever do to deserve being Public Enemy Number One of Brooklawne High?

I wish I could take Sammy of a few weeks ago who was so freaked out about exams and prom and shake her by the shoulders and say, "Really, Samantha? You think this is something to stress about? Get a grip, girl, 'cause you ain't seen *nothin'* yet!"

I wonder if that Sammy would listen to me. I wonder if she'd do anything different.

Probably not. Real *now* problems are always more pressing than theoretical *future* ones, even if they are smaller and less important.

Or else maybe it's that people aren't good at listening.

Maybe *I'm* just not good at listening.

Maybe I need to try listening more.

Maybe then I'll hear what's actually going on in my own house so I don't have to learn it from hackers.

Noah looks up from the screen and calls my name when I get to the media center for my open. I'd planned to avoid him, because I'm so mortified that he's read about my ridiculous unrequited lusting over Jamie Moss and seen how well that turned out for me. I can't even imagine what he must think of me. Actually, I can. He must think I'm the World's Biggest Idiot.

I go over, waiting for him to say something to that effect. "Hey, Noah. What's up?"

"I don't know," he says. "I was wondering if I should feel offended."

"Why would you feel offended?" I ask, confused. I'm sure I didn't say anything bad about him in my journal. I don't even think I wrote anything about him at all. At least not the part that went public.

"Because I don't feature much in your diary."

I stare at him, wondering if he's lost his marbles. "Why would you *want* to be in my diary?"

"Because if I was in your diary, it would mean that I actually registered on your radar," Noah explains with a wry grin. "And since I wasn't, maybe I'm nothing more than a butler to you."

His words are like a gut punch, for two reasons.

1. Because he's read my diary. Total. Mortification.
2. Because he's right.

Not that he was invisible, exactly, but he's floated around on the fringes of my life until skipping out together the day of the first data dump brought us closer together.

Maybe becoming better friends with Noah is an example of finding an "opportunity in my difficulty."

"You were never invisible. We've shared classes since middle school," I tell him. "I guess maybe I can just see you better now. Maybe I should have had my eyes checked."

It's hard to admit that I've been walking around so wrapped up and blind to things, but Noah's answering smile makes it worth it. I'm also relieved that he doesn't offer an opinion on my poor choice in potential prom dates.

Until he says: "So . . . I gather you're not a big fan of the promposal, huh?"

I hide my face behind a curtain of curls. "Can we *not* talk about prom?" I beg. "That's pretty much my least favorite topic right now—besides hackers and cancer."

"Sammy, I'm so sorry" he says. "Is . . . your mom going to be okay?"

I shift my hair and look into his eyes, which seem to show genuine concern, not just a quest for the latest gossip.

"I don't know for sure," I whisper. "That's the most awful part of this. Even worse than the hackers and the humiliation. And I'm supposed to try to be positive for my mom's sake, but it's not easy when my friends won't talk to me and it feels like everyone can see in my head."

"I'll bet," Noah says. "Well . . . my head's a pretty freaky place. I wouldn't want everyone to see what's there. Isn't that why you choose what to show people?"

"I didn't choose this," I correct him. "Now everyone hates me or thinks I'm a moron."

"Not everyone hates you and thinks you're a moron, Sammy," Noah says. "For example, me."

"Yay! You make one!" I observe. "And BethAnn Jackson doesn't. That makes a grand total of two people in a school of fifteen hundred kids who don't hate me or think I'm an idiot! Woo-hoo!"

"There are more, Sammy," Noah says. "It's just the haters are always louder."

"I guess," I admit. "If it weren't for the hackers, BethAnn wouldn't have known that I hated what Gary did to her."

"*I* hate what the hackers have done to *you*," Noah says.

"But you read my journal anyway," I point out. "You could have chosen not to. Couldn't you have left me with a few shreds of dignity?"

He looks away, and a flush tints his cheeks. "I'm sorry," he says. "I knew I shouldn't. It's just . . ." He looks me straight in the eye. "It gave me a chance to know you better, and I couldn't help myself from taking it."

His face turns another shade redder with this admission.

"How is that fair?" I ask. "Now you've seen the inside of my head, but yours is still a mystery to me. Do you know what it feels like to walk around feeling like everyone knows everything?"

"Awful," he says. "Unbearable."

"Yeah, and that's when it's people you don't even know who are judging you. It's even worse when it's your friends."

"I'm not judging you, Sammy," Noah says. "In fact, I . . ." He hesitates, and looks down at his hands.

"In fact, you what?"

"I was hoping that *you'd* want to see into my head as much as I wanted to see into yours. Because . . . I really like you. And, um . . ." He looks up and gives me a shy smile. "I was wondering if you wanted to go to prom with me."

I'm surprised into speechlessness. Just when I thought today was the worst day of my life, a spark of hope and awesomeness blossoms inside as I picture being at prom with Noah.

Unfortunately, Noah takes my stunned silence the wrong way.

"I know I'm not Jamie Moss, and he's the guy you really wanted to go with," he says, getting redder in the face than I thought was possible unless you were a lobster in a pot, being prepared for dinner. "But I figured maybe I could be a halfway decent runner-up . . . you know, if you want to go, that is. But if you don't, it's okay, I'll understand. I mean—"

"Yes."

"What?"

"Yes," I repeat.

"Really?" he asks, an adorable smile slowly spreading across his face.

"Well, there is a slight catch."

The smile dims a bit. "There always is," he says.

"I'm grounded," I confess.

"That's more than slight," Noah says.

"But my dad said I could maybe earn my way back into going," I tell him. "If I stop breaking all the rules."

"Can you do it, Sammy?" he teases. "Can you stop breaking the rules? For me?"

I laugh. "I said yes, didn't I? And it's not like I was such a rebel before all this happened. I messed up once—okay, like three times now that I skipped out with you the other day and then cut school the day after they dumped my journal. But my mom agreed to count that as a mental health day. I think I can handle being good for a few weeks."

"Even with school being . . . not so great?"

"Like Sir Winston Churchill said . . ." I put on my best Winnie imitation, which is nowhere as good as my dad's. "'We shall draw from the heart of suffering itself the means of inspiration and survival.'"

Noah slow-claps. "Impressive," he says. His face has gone back to its natural hue and he's smiling as if he's just snagged the prize in the cereal box. "So I guess I've got a date. Maybe."

"Definitely maybe," I agree.

In fairy tales, this is where the story would fade to black. All's well that ends well, because I finally have a date with the handsome, if somewhat shy and geeky, prince. But clearly, my life is no fairy tale. Instead, the only thing that's changing slightly is the way I'm trying to look at the situation I'm in. It's not just because of Noah and the prom date. It's just as much because BethAnn made me realize that the hackers exposing my journal made *her* feel less alone.

I mean, don't get me wrong. I'm still pissed about the hacking and my mom's cancer and the crash-and-burn of my social life. But at least I'm able to see there are some silver linings in this very dark cloud, even though I'm still stuck in the middle of it. I just have to keep looking for them.

#InspirationAndSurvival, yeah?

Everyone dreads Monday morning, and the thought of going back to school tomorrow is making me feel physically ill. It's so not helping that every day, the news has another story about New Territories Bank because of something else the hackers have revealed. How long is it going to be this way?

I actually found myself wishing for a huge natural disaster somewhere else that would wipe this off the front page. But then I realize how awful and selfish that is, because innocent people would be injured and die, and I don't want that to happen just to make my life better.

So I've been trying to think about the good things. Like a hot prom date, even though I'm grounded, so going is still up in the air. What's weird about it is how excited I am about going with Noah—and I didn't even have to survive the awkwardness of being promposed to in front of the whole school. It just happened.

And while people I thought were my best friends, Margo and Rosa, ditched me, others who I wouldn't have expected to be supportive, are. Like on Friday, I was sitting by myself at lunch because Margo and Rosa aren't talking to me. They weren't even sitting with each other. I think Rosa is pissed at Margo now that she knows Margo let her mom think Rosa had been drinking the night of the Einstein's Encounter concert. But I can't be sure, because she's not talking to me.

Anyway, I was sitting by myself, feeling miserable and mad. Mad because even though I know I wrote some things I shouldn't have in my PRIVATE journal, you'd think that maybe my friends might have given me a break when they found out my mom has cancer. Or at least stopped giving me the cold shoulder long enough to ask how she is and how I'm handling that on top of everything else.

Nope. They're just pretending I don't exist.

I know, I know. Pity party, table for one.

But then BethAnn came over and asked me if I wanted to sit with her and her friends.

"Are you sure you want to risk being seen with me?" I asked her. "I'm Public Enemy Number One right now."

"Been there, done that, got the Wanted poster," she said. "Come on, join us."

So I took my lunch and went to sit with BethAnn and her friends. No one mentioned the news stories about my dad. But Omar Karim asked me how my mom was doing and Valerie Chen asked me how I was holding up. There was a lump in my throat that had nothing to do with my sandwich.

Maybe it's moments like that where I'm supposed to find the inspiration at the heart of my suffering. Kindness and friendship when you least expect it.

THIRTEEN

"So, are you excited?" BethAnn asks me at lunch. "Today's D-Day!"

"If I pass that is," I say.

"I passed," Omar points out. "And I was so nervous that I thought my shaking foot wouldn't be able to press on the brake pedal."

"I did, too," Valerie says. "And I had the meanest examiner ever."

"Don't tell me that," I beg her. "I'm nervous about taking my driving test without the thought of mean examiners!"

"Come on, guys, stop freaking her out," BethAnn says. "Don't worry, Sammy. You'll be fine."

"I *need* to pass my test," I tell them. "Before, it was just about freedom and independence. But now . . . I have to be able to drive to help out when my mom . . ." I don't finish.

"You'll pass," Valerie says. "It'll be okay."

I wish I believed her. I have to force myself to get out of bed and go to school every day. It's hard to believe that anything is going to be okay again, ever.

"So did you guys get your prom tickets yet?" Omar asks, looking over where they've been selling tickets every lunch period. He's obviously trying to change the subject.

"Ugh!" BethAnn exclaims. "Don't even talk to me about prom."

"Well, I got asked, but I'm not sure I can go because I'm grounded," I admit.

"Whaaaat? Who?!" Valerie exclaims. "When was the promposal?"

"No fancy promposal," I say. "Just a simple ask."

"But who?" BethAnn says.

"Noah," I say.

"Noah Woods?" Omar asks.

I nod shyly.

"Cool," he says.

"But like I said, I'm not sure if I can even go," I say. "I have to earn back the privilege."

"It's a lot of money," Omar says. "Especially for someone like me, who would rather be put in a tank with a hungry great white shark than go on a dance floor. I mean you have to buy the tickets, rent a tux, get a limo, buy the pictures . . ."

"You forgot the corsage," BethAnn reminds him.

"Oh yeah, that," Omar groans. "I forgot about that."

"And the girl has to buy a boutonniere. And a dress," Valerie points out.

"I don't even want to go to prom after how everyone treated me like a pariah when I told Gary Harvey I wasn't going with him," BethAnn says. "I hate the whole thing now."

The idea hits me suddenly. "What if we had our own prom?"

They all stare at me.

"What do you mean?" Valerie asks.

"I mean we could have our own mini prom," I explain, making it up as I go along. "Like we could call it . . . Faux Prom. For when the real prom is too fake."

BethAnn laughs. "Now, that sounds like a plan with a capital *P*."

"We could make it as understated as the real prom is over-stated," I say. "Like we'd agree: no renting tuxes, get your dresses and jackets at Goodwill—"

"No limos!" Omar says.

"No corsages or boutonnieres," Valerie suggests. "What's the point of wearing a bunch of flowers on your wrist?"

"I know, right?" BethAnn agrees. "It looks so dorky. But everyone does it anyway."

"Because that's what *their* parents did," I point out.

"And that's what *their* parents did," Valerie says.

"And that's what their parents and their *parents'* parents did before that, and so on and so on back into the fog of time," BethAnn says. "Why do we do these same rituals the same way, generation after generation? Why can't we change things up a bit?"

"No good reason that I can think of," Valerie says. "It is hereby agreed that we refuse to continue the time-honored prom ritual of wearing corsages on our wrists, because we no longer see the point. If there was any point to begin with."

"This has epic potential," BethAnn says. "I'll ask my parents if we can have it at my house. My aunt Julie says it's got 'great flow for parties,' and she's in real estate, so she knows about that stuff."

I wonder if my parents will be any more or less likely to let me go to a Faux Prom than the actual prom. Either way, I have to keep on being a model child so I can earn the right. The other wild card is Noah. He asked me to the real prom. I wonder how he would feel about a change in plan.

Noah meets me at my locker right before I leave to take my driving test.

"Good luck," he says. "Text me."

"I will," I promise. "Listen, can I ask you something?"

"It's a free country," he says. "Shoot."

I feel nervous asking, but then I realize it took more guts for Noah to ask me. He thought I liked some other guy. So I force myself to say, "How would you feel about not going to prom?"

As soon as the words are out of my mouth and I see the

hurt expression on his face, I realize that I've just made a whopping great big mistake.

"Wait! That came out wrong. I don't mean *not go together*," I hasten to explain. "I mean not go to the official prom."

"Oh!" Noah's body seems to release a tension I didn't even realize it was holding and he smiles in obvious relief. "I thought you were blowing me off. You know, that you'd got a better offer or something."

Guys have always seemed like a foreign country, speaking a different language, inscrutable and often incomprehensible. But by letting me know that he's just as insecure as I am, Noah's just given me a piece of the Rosetta stone.

"Of course not," I reassure him. "I want to go with you. I'm working hard to be good so I can. Can't you see my halo?"

He searches over my head. "I think you might have to work a little harder. It's a bit dim."

I mock-glare at him. "Just wait till I pass my driving test," I say. "*If* I pass my driving test . . ."

"You will," he says, putting his arm around me and giving me an encouraging hug. I feel tingles where his hand touches my arm, which I don't think have anything to do with static electricity. "So tell me. What are we doing if we aren't going to the official prom?"

"Oh! So at lunch we got to talking about prom. BethAnn doesn't want to go after how people treated her, and Omar was complaining about the cost."

"Yeah, it is pretty pricey, when you start adding it all up," Noah admits. "Not that you aren't worth it."

I laugh and strike a pose. Then say, "Well, what if we made our own prom? One that we did our own way? That's the idea we had."

A wide grin spreads over Noah's face. "I like it," he says. "And luckily, I didn't buy prom tickets yet since we're waiting on your pending parole."

"Great!" I say. Glancing up at the wall clock, I realize my mom's going to be waiting for me. "I've got to go or I'll be late for my driving test."

"Break a leg," he says.

"Um, maybe not," I say, laughing as I walk away down the hall. "'Cause that would make it pretty much impossible to pass my driving test!"

April 17

Guess who is now the owner of a shiny new driver's license! Yours truly, that's who. I always thought that when I got my license, the first thing I'd do would be to take a drive to Rosa's, then Margo's. Then we'd just drive around for hours, blasting music and rocking out. But they've both ditched me. I'm pretty much dead to Margo, although she doesn't hesitate to trash-talk me whenever she can. Rosa's not saying anything bad—she's just not saying anything at all. At least not to me. So to celebrate my licensed driver status I ended up driving Mom to Lickety Splits and celebrating with ice cream. Mom only clutched the door handle once the whole time, and we didn't fight about my driving at all! Imagine that! Proof that miracles can happen . . .

I was actually feeling really happy until Jamie and Geneva walked in. I told Mom I wanted to leave and she said not until she finished her ice cream and I said, "Please, Mom, can we just go now," and she wouldn't, so I said I was going to go wait in the car and left, because I wanted to try to hold on to the feeling of happiness for a few more minutes and I couldn't if I was watching Jamie and Geneva hold hands and make out over ice cream. Gross.

Why did it even hurt so much? I was an idiot to think that Jamie would ever invite me to the prom. He just wanted me for my homework. (If Margo or Rosa were talking to me, I might be forced to admit they were right . . .)

It would have been bad enough if I had to know that in private. But my public humiliation is way worse.

Mom yelled at me when she got in the car. She told me I was rude and selfish and when your mom buys you an ice cream, the least you can do is have the courtesy to sit with her until she's finished.

But then she noticed I was staring at the center of the steering wheel and she asked me what was going on. And I looked into the window of Lickety Splits and Jamie and Geneva were kissing, which set me off again. Mom followed my gaze and asked, "Wait. Is that Jamie Moss, the lacrosse guy?" I nodded and she said, "Oh no, baby," and pulled me into her arms. And I cried and cried, and she stroked my hair and said that he wasn't good enough for me, and I said, "I know he isn't, he's a jerk, but he's still really cute."

And then Mom started laughing and so did I, but I was crying at the same time, so snot came out of my nose, which was really disgusting and it got on Mom's shirt, which I thought would have her freaking, but she was like, "Is this going to be your new thing? Destroying my clothes?"

I said it was cheaper than destroying the car, and she said, "I can't argue with that. I know it's hard, honey, but forget that cute jerk, sweetheart. As Grandma Sally used to say to me, 'There are plenty of fish in the sea.' And given how much you like sushi, I'm sure you'll find a more suitable fish soon."

I was like, "Seriously, Mom? You're comparing boys to sushi? No wonder you and Dad get along so well—because you're both ridiculously weird. He told me my hair smelled like vacation once."

"That's my Richard." She laughed, and said, "Come on, Sammy the Chauffeur. If you've finished sliming me with snot, you can drive me home."

Mom even let me listen to my favorite Sirius station and sang along with a few songs.

I guess I managed to hold on to some happiness after all.

FOURTEEN

BethAnn's parents agreed to let her host our Faux Prom the night of real prom.

"They were so happy I wanted to anything remotely related to a high school dance ritual after the whole Gary incident that they even offered to pay for food and decorations," she tells me.

"We can all chip in," I offer. "We would have had to pay for a prom ticket anyway."

"Let's see how many people are coming," BethAnn says. "If it's not a lot of people, my parents will be cool with it. What else do you think we need, though?"

"Music, obviously," Omar says. "I'm happy to DJ. Anything that means I don't have to, yanno, *dance*."

"But if you don't dance, you won't play dance music," Valerie complains.

"That's a complete fallacy," Omar argues. "I have a healthy appreciation of dance music. I just don't want to stand in the middle of the floor, throwing my arms and legs around like an amphibian having convulsions."

I burst out laughing at the mental picture, but Valerie still looks skeptical. "I know your taste in music, and it's not what *I* usually dance to."

"How about everyone makes a playlist as the price of admission?" I suggest.

"Or something else to contribute to the festive atmosphere if music isn't your thing," BethAnn says. "Because the whole point is for this to be the no-pressure, no-stress prom."

"Sounds good to me," I sigh. "I've got more than enough stress with AP exams next week."

"I feel ya," Valerie says.

"Don't we all," Omar groans.

"Yeah, but Sammy's got stress on steroids because of her mom," Valerie points out.

"But I passed my driving test!" I remind them. "One test down, only . . . like a zillion more to go!"

"I'm going to start a closed Faux Prom group so we can send invites out," BethAnn says. "And I'll make all you guys admins, too."

"Uh . . . I don't think you should make me an admin," I tell her. "What if I get hacked again?"

BethAnn laughs. "You're probably the safest one out of all of us now. Your entire life already went viral. Besides, didn't your dad get a security expert?"

"Yeah," I admit. "But still . . . if I've learned anything from this, we're never really safe."

"No worries, Sammy. We're talking about a party, not our social security numbers," BethAnn points out. "Even if you do get hacked again, what are they going to do? Point out that we didn't go to prom and had our own party? Call us losers? Boo-hoo! Compared to what's already been said about me online, that's nothing."

She's probably right. But I guess I'm still feeling Internet shy. We all have our public faces, the things about ourselves that we choose to reveal to the world. But like Mom says, everyone has secrets. They don't have to be embarrassing, dark, or evil, just our little private pieces of self.

Is never expressing those thoughts, even using writing as a way to work out your feelings, or as a stress valve, the only way to guarantee that they won't be made public, ever?

Is the only private place left inside my head?

Because if that's the case, what do I do when my head is so filled with fears and anxiety that it feels like it's about to shatter into a million tiny shards?

Writing is what helps me make sense of the world. It's a safe bucket where I can vomit my feelings when they're so intense they're making me sick and dizzy.

I can't give it up, even knowing the risks. I just have to figure out how to adapt.

It took many calls by Mom's surgeon to the insurance company, but they managed to move up her surgery date since everyone on the Internet knows she has cancer. I told my parents there was no point in waiting till I was done with APs to reduce my stress.

"It would be better to get it over with," Mom agreed. "Thinking about those cancer cells growing and dividing inside me is horrible. I want them out sooner rather than later."

My dad takes Mom to the hospital the night before the surgery for prep because the operation is early in the morning. I want to go, but Mom won't let me, because my first AP, English Lit, is tomorrow.

"You need to focus on *your* job, which is doing well on your exams, and I need to focus on *my* job, which is kicking this cancer," she says.

"I'm postmillennial, Mom," I tell her. "I was born knowing how to multitask."

Dad looks at Mom, and the two of them start laughing.

"You think you have it bad, Helene? This is what I deal with from bright young sparks at work *every single day.*"

"Yeah, *whatever*, old man," I tease. "Should I get your cane so you can wave it when you get mad?"

"Okay, she's definitely staying home," Dad says. "She called me *old man*."

"If the shoe fits, Dad . . ." RJ says.

Dad ruffles my brother's hair. "*Et tu*, RJ? Help me, Helene—the kids are ganging up on their old dad!"

"Emphasis on *old*," I say. It's nice to be joking with my dad again in this moment. This is the dad I know. Not the guy in the newspapers. Dad's still living at the office these days, coming home early only for doctors' appointments with Mom. And sometimes it's so easy to slip into this comforting familiarity and forget that I'm mad about all the other stuff. But I can't. Because I need to know who the real Richard M. Wallach is. Is it this dad, or the one in the emails?

"Don't look at me, Dick," Mom replies. "I'm having an operation tomorrow. You're on your own, honey."

We all will be while she's in the hospital, though hopefully not longer than that. Hopefully not forever.

"Okay, let's go," Dad tells Mom. "I need to escape before I lose my self-respect entirely."

Mom gives RJ a hug, and then me.

"Good luck tomorrow," she says.

I don't want to let go. I know people get mastectomies all the time. I know from the online research I've done that the survival rate for the stage cancer Mom has is 93 percent, which are way better odds than I ever really had of Jamie Moss asking me to prom. As much as I thought prom mattered to me, it doesn't even register compared to how much Mom matters. She can't be in the 7 percent. She just can't.

"Don't worry, Sammy," she whispers, as if she can read my mind. "I'm going to be fine."

"I know," I say, even though the number seven weaves itself in my brain like Kaa in *The Jungle Book*.

She kisses my forehead and then bends down to say goodbye to Scruffles.

"Keep a good eye on my babies for me, Scruffs, okay?"

Scruffles licks her face, but his tail is between his legs. He knows she's leaving, and it makes him sad, too.

After Mom and Dad walk out to the garage, I give him a treat.

"Don't worry, Scruffles. Mom's coming back."

"Is she really going to be okay?" RJ asks.

I have to push the python seven out of my head and try to believe in odds of ninety-three enough to sound convincing for my brother.

"She will, RJ," I tell him. "Hey, do you want some ice cream? I need something to keep me going for studying."

He nods, and we watch the Science Channel and eat ice cream, with Scruffles curled on the sofa between us, until I have to force myself back to my books.

I've done two rounds with the flash cards when I get a text from BethAnn.

think the parental units are more into faux prom than we are! they just came back from home depot with enough boxes of fairy lights that orbiting satellites should be able to see our yard!

I love that her parents are so into the alternative prom we're throwing. I haven't asked my parents about going yet. We've all been so preoccupied with Mom's cancer. But helping to plan it keeps me distracted from the number seven.

awesome. what can i do?

study for your APs and take care of your mom, BethAnn texts me. valerie, noah, and omar are helping with stuff. you don't have to do anything unless you feel like it, okay? we've got this.

After all the whispers and the stares, after getting the cold shoulder from my best friends, knowing that there are people in my life who care brings a lump to my throat.

thanks. <3 I text back.

wait. you DO have to get an outfit of some kind from goodwill. clothes are NOT optional. :p

I laugh out loud. For real.

When Dad gets back from the hospital, my brother and I go down to get a report on Mom.

"She settled in well," Dad tells us. "She sends her love and said to tell you not to worry."

RJ looks at me and rolls his eyes. "Yeah, like *that's* a possibility," he says.

The kid has a point, one that even Dad is forced to acknowledge.

"Asking you not to worry is unreasonable," he admits. "How about we just try to keep the worry in check the best we can. Because the prognosis is really good."

Or as good as it can be for cancer.

"I'll get you guys off to school in the morning, then go to the hospital," Dad says. "Mom will be in surgery by then."

"You should be there before she goes into surgery to give her moral support," I tell him. "RJ and I can handle getting ourselves to school, right?"

RJ nods. "Definitely. You should be at the hospital."

Dad hesitates. I know he wants to be with Mom, but he probably promised her that he'd be here looking after us.

"But your AP exams start tomorrow, Sammy," he says. "I don't want you to have any additional stress."

RJ gives me an *Is he serious?* glance, and I snort.

"Dad, the Additional Stress Train left the station three

weeks ago," I tell him. "We can handle getting up and eating breakfast, right, RJ?"

"With our eyes closed," RJ agrees. "Go keep Mom company."

Dad relaxes, visibly. "Okay, if you're sure. Mom's putting on a brave face, but I know it'll make her feel better not being alone."

He gathers us for a group hug. "It'll make me feel better to be there, too."

We stand in his embrace, both giving and drawing comfort as we offer silent prayers for a good outcome.

I text Mom a selfie of RJ, Scruffles, and me doing a thumbs-up before I leave for school, even though I know she's already in surgery. Well, Scruffles isn't doing the thumbs-up; he's doing paws-up. I write:

we got dressed, ate breakfast, and left for school ALL BY OURSELVES :) we LOVE YOU. :x :x :x

Who knows when she'll see it? But at least she'll know we're thinking of her and that everything went okay.

The AP starts at seven thirty. Even though we're normally in school this early, it seems like cruel and unusual punishment to have to take a test that really matters for college at this time in the morning. So much for the research that says teenagers need more sleep. Why let science get in the way of Very Important Tests?

I watch the clock throughout the exam, but it's only partially to pace myself for the test. All I want is for the exam to be over so I can get outside, turn on my cell, and see if Dad sent an update on Mom.

Focus on the test. Pretend you're in a tunnel where your sole focus is English lit.

NO. Not the tunnel where there's a white light at the end like when you're dying! AAAAAAH!

I was getting 4s and 5s on the practice tests before I found out about the cancer. At this rate, I'll be lucky to get a 3. But it's okay. What's the worst thing that can happen if I don't do well on the AP? I go to a different college, or don't get credit.

That's nothing compared to what's the worst thing that could happen if . . .

The test, Sammy!!! The test!

Finally it's over and we're allowed to leave the room. I race out and turn on my cell. There's a text from Dad saying Mom went in, she was in positive spirits, and she sends her love. But nothing else.

So I text him.

what's happening? any news?

Still in the OR, he texts back.

is that bad? I ask.

It's neither good nor bad. It just is.

what's that supposed to mean, yoda?

It means, try not to worry (yeah, I know). I'll text you as soon as there's news. Love, Dad.

He *still* hasn't learned that when we're texting, I know it's him. But given the circumstances, I let it slide.

The second hand of the clock on the classroom wall appears to be moving through thick sludge. I think it's broken. There's a sign taped above it that says: "Time passes. Will you?" Not that they're trying to put added stress on us or anything. I take out my cell and check a minute against the clock. Nope, it's working—it's my perception of time that isn't. Still, it's hard not to keep watching the clock when all I care about is when I'm going to get the text from Dad telling me that Mom's okay.

I don't even know why we have to pretend to be learning anything anyway. Schedules are so messed up because of APs.

Some schools let you go home after you've taken AP exams because they realize your brain is fried, but not our school. Here at Brooklawne High, the message is *Achieve, achieve, achieve! Got to keep those college admissions up!*

It's not till almost twelve thirty that I get a text from Dad saying that Mom's in the recovery room. How can they have operated on her for that long?

The doctors say she's doing okay, but that they had to take out several lymph nodes because it had spread.

Does that mean her probability of survival is less than 93 percent? Why can't he be more specific?

When I text him back to ask, he says he'll explain more later, when he sees us at the hospital. I'm going to drive RJ so we can both visit without Dad having to leave Mom's side.

I think it's cruel of him to make me wait.

Scruffles practically knocks me over in his excitement to see me. Our next-door neighbor Mrs. Maxon came over to let him out during the day, but he gets lonely when he's by himself for long periods.

"You're a people dog, aren't you, Scruffs?" I tell him. He jumps up to lick my nose with such enthusiasm that he almost gives me a nosebleed.

After letting him out and getting a snack, I take out my book to study for the AP exam tomorrow, but who am I kidding? I have to read the same sentence three times because I just want to go to the hospital, and where on earth is RJ?

Why isn't his bus here yet? I should have just picked him up from school.

When he finally does walk in the door, I practically shovel a snack down his throat and say, "Come on, let's go!"

"Can I at least go to the bathroom first?" he asks. "Or are you going to make me pee in a bottle in the car so we can leave *right this very minute.*"

"I'm sorry," I say. "I guess I'm getting a little over the top, huh?"

"*A little?*"

"Hurry up. I'll be waiting in the car," I tell him.

We stop at the local florist to pick up flowers, tulips from me and daisies from RJ, and then continue on to the hospital. Dad's warned us that Mom might still be kind of out of it because of the painkillers, so we shouldn't expect to have any deep and meaningful conversations—she might well be asleep.

Just as the elevator door closes to go up to her room at the hospital, RJ blurts out, "What if she looks totally different?"

I squeeze his shoulder gently.

"I don't think she'll look that different yet. She said she probably won't lose her hair until a few weeks after the first round of chemo," I tell him. "Anyway, she'll still look better bald than Grandpa Marty does."

"But one of her . . . you know . . . *things* is missing."

"*Things?* You mean breasts?"

RJ blushes fifty shades of pink. "SAMMY! Stop it!"

"It's a biological term, bro. Hashtag science," I tell him. "And Mom's still Mom. She's not defined by her *things*."

"I know, but she's going to look different."

"So? Do you think she'd love you any less if you got your arm caught in this elevator door and it had to be amputated?"

"No," RJ admits, shrinking back as far as he can from the elevator door.

Nice work, Sammy. He'll probably have nightmares tonight.

"Anyway, Mom's having reconstructive surgery, so she'll have two breasts eventually. This is just temporary."

As long as she's not one of the 7 percent.

RJ still looks nervous when the elevator door opens, although I'm not sure if that's because he's more afraid of his arm getting caught and having to be amputated (me and my brilliant analogies) or seeing Mom.

I go into the room, but RJ stops in the doorway, reluctant to enter.

Grandma Sally and Dad are sitting on either side of Mom's bed. Mom rests against the pillows, her face slack with exhaustion—or maybe it's the painkillers. White bandages peep out through the neck of her nightgown, as if waving to remind us there's something missing. There's an enormous flower arrangement on the windowsill. It's so big it practically blocks out the light.

"Sammy!" she says, holding out the arm on the opposite side from the operation.

I go to hug her, tentatively because I'm afraid to hurt her. She smells of hospital. I want her to smell like my mom again.

"These are for you," I tell her, handing her the flowers.

"So pretty," Mom says. "Thank you."

"I'll go get a vase," Grandma says, getting up from the chair. "Come, Sammy, take my seat. I need to stretch my old legs anyway."

RJ's still standing in the doorway, as immovable as one of the presidents carved on Mount Rushmore.

Grandma Sally kisses him on the cheek and then gives him a gentle push toward the bed as she walks into the hallway in search of vases.

"Hey, honey," Mom says to him. "How was your day?"

"Better than yours, I guess," RJ mumbles. He sticks out the flowers from a foot away. "I brought these for you."

"I love daisies," Mom says. "They're cheerful faces of sunshine."

RJ's looking anywhere but at Mom. It's so obvious she's got to notice.

"Our flowers are kind of lame compared to that," I say, pointing to the massive arrangement on the window. "Are they from Dad?"

Mom smiles. "No. Those are from Grandma Gertie. You know Grandma G. She never does anything by halves."

"Yeah," I say, nodding. "Good thing you don't get hay fever."

"I love your flowers," Mom says. "They're simple and beautiful, and most of all because they're from you."

"How'd the AP test go, Sammy?" Dad asks, clearly wanting to change the subject.

RJ uses that deflection of attention to edge farther away from our mom. Judging by the almost imperceptible frown and the slight wrinkle in her brow, I think she realizes what's going on.

"I think I did okay," I say, keeping my eyes on Mom's face.

"Just okay?" Dad says.

"Well, I was finding it harder than usual to focus for some strange reason," I point out, turning to Dad with a frown.

"Let's not talk about tests," Mom pleads in a weak voice. "Let's just be here. Together." She smiles at me. "Both Sammy and I have had tests out the wazoo."

Grandma Sally, who has just walked back in the door with two vases, asks, "What's this about wazoos?" She notices that RJ has edged almost all the way back to the door. "RJ, how about you help me arrange these flowers?"

"Sure!" My brother rushes to assist, even though flower arranging isn't usually high—or more like anywhere—on his list of things to do. But it gives him a reason not to look at Mom.

"When are you coming home?" I ask Mom.

"I'm not sure," she says. "I'll know more tomorrow, after we see the surgeons again."

No one offers an answer to the question I really want to ask. As long as I don't ask the question, Mom can be both in the 93 percent and/or the 7 percent group of breast cancer patients. But if I ask the question, and she's in the 7 percent, then she's going to die. I refuse to be responsible for the death of my mom by opening my mouth to ask the question.

So I just smile and pretend that I'm not worrying so much that my stomach hurts, trying to give Mom comfort until it's time to go home to study for the next day's AP exam.

May 4

Mom is home—they let her out two days after surgery. She has these weird tubes for drainage that have to be emptied and the fluid measured to report to the doctor. Dad helps do it when he's home, but then they asked me if I'd be okay helping her do it when he's not, otherwise they'd ask Grandma to come over, or one of Mom's friends.

"It's okay to say no if it freaks you out," Mom said.

How could it NOT freak me out? I mean, seriously . . . There are these TUBES sticking out of my mom's BODY with gross bodily fluids in them. EW. EW. EW and MORE EW!!!

Not to mention the fact that because of the Internet research I've done about breast cancer, I now know that because Mom's had it, I'm at higher risk of going through all this "fun" myself someday.

YAY GENETICS!

But despite being completely grossed out, I said yes, because what else would I say? She's my mom and I'm going to do whatever it takes to make sure she stays in the 93 percent group. Being freaked out is a relatively small price to pay, if you look at it that way.

It's better than death.

FIFTEEN

Two APs down. Two more to go. I've taken time during study breaks to work on my Faux Prom playlist. It feels like I'm getting to the top of the mountain, and soon I'll be able to see the view of summer and fun and relaxation—unless, of course, the view turns out to be another mountain to climb.

Oops. Clearly, I haven't quite got this *Think Positively* thing down to a science yet.

Mom's still pretty doped up on painkillers. She spends a lot of time resting and napping. Dad's been trying to work from home, but on Friday the hackers released another round of documents, so he had to go in and deal with damage control. He's been at work most of the weekend. Grandma Sally and Grandpa Marty have been coming over to help, but they had to go to a wedding today, the daughter of one of Grandpa's clients. Grandma offered to stay, but I know Grandpa well enough to know that he'd be miserable if he had to go by himself. Mom agreed.

I told them it was fine, that RJ and I have things under control.

Actually, Scruffles has been more help than RJ. He hasn't left Mom's side since she got home. Even when she goes to the bathroom, Scruffles waits outside the door until she comes out. It's like he knows she's hurting and needs the comfort of his presence.

I'm studying downstairs when Mom texts me from her room.

Can you come help me empty the drains?

Even though it's the last thing I want to do, I text back, **sure, coming!**

I dread doing this, even though I know it's important. Seeing the stuff that's coming through the tubes and having to measure it. Having to look at it to see if it's turning from red blood into more straw colored . . . yuck. These are things that I shouldn't have to think about and I *definitely* shouldn't have to look at with my sensitive teenage eyes. I'm probably going to be traumatized for life because of this.

But I paste on my best positive smile and walk through the bedroom door.

"Ready for the drain train?" I say.

"Ready as I'll ever be," Mom replies.

I'm half gagging so many times during the process, but trying to hide it from my mom because I don't want her to feel bad. She can't help what's happening to her body. And if this is what is going to make her better, then I just have to deal, as much as it freaks and grosses me out.

From the way my mom's wincing, I know she's trying to hide how much it hurts her from me, too.

"Are you okay?" I ask.

"I'm fine," she says. "But I'll be really happy when they take these things out."

"Yeah. I bet," I say. I write down the volume of liquid on the drainage log and then look up at her face and see her lips tight from trying to keep in any expression of pain. "Mom, it's okay to say it hurts. It's not like it's a big secret or anything."

She exhales, heavily. "I didn't want to scare you," she says. "It's hard enough for you already."

"It's less scary if you're honest than if you pretend," I tell her. "News flash: not a little kid anymore."

Mom smiles, her eyes really lighting up for the first time all day. "How could I possibly miss that?" she says. "You're a funny, smart, incredible young woman and I'm proud as anything to be your mother."

I can't help but smile—even when the next thing she says is: "Okay, I confess. I am ready for my next painkiller because that hurt like crazy."

The pitcher on her nightstand is empty, so I shout to RJ, asking him to refill it while I help Mom get settled more comfortably. He shouts back that he's in the middle of something. What could be so important that he can't do one little thing to help Mom? He's been completely useless. Less than useless. Meanwhile, I've had to do everything. Story of my life.

I help Mom get the pillows just the way she likes them and then get the water myself.

"Here you go," I say, giving her the painkillers and a full glass.

She grasps my hand as she takes the glass from me. "Thanks, sweetheart. Love you."

"Love you, too, Mom," I tell her, and then leave her to rest with Scruffles curled up beside her, his head resting on her thigh.

I close her door, leaving it slightly ajar so I can hear if she calls me, and then go to see what RJ is so busy doing.

I can't believe my eyes. The little twerp is playing Minecraft.

"Is this a joke?" I ask, barely able to contain my fury. "You couldn't help get Mom more water because you're in the middle of *playing a video game*?"

My brother doesn't even take his eyes off the screen. "Yeah. So?"

"What's wrong with you?" I ask, unable to believe my brother is this much of a jerk. "Don't you even *care*?"

He doesn't say a word, just keeps on playing his stupid game. I start to leave the room, thinking what a self-centered little brat he is, when I remember how freaked out he was when we visited Mom in the hospital.

So I turn back.

"I'm scared, too, you know," I tell him. "Maybe it doesn't seem like it to you, but that's because I'm sucking it up and doing the best I can because Mom needs us right now. She needs us a lot. We need to be there for her like she's always been there for us, even if things freak us out." I take a deep breath to give him time to let that sink in and release the nuclear option. "At least you don't have to help Mom empty those drains. Consider yourself lucky."

His fingers stop moving on the keyboard for a moment, but he still doesn't turn around. When he starts typing again, I leave before I say something I know I'll regret.

But when I go upstairs to check on Mom two hours later, RJ is sitting on the bed next to her and Scruffles, reading to her from his independent reading book. Even though Mom's eyes are closed, she has a smile on her face.

On Sunday afternoon, Dad's at work again, surprise, surprise. I'm starting to understand why Mom gets so frustrated now that I have to be responsible for everything because she's recuperating and he's not here. She's lying on the sofa in the family room resting and watching TV while I study in the kitchen and try to figure out what to make for dinner. It's such a pain having to think about dinner, much less make it. I don't know how Mom does it all the time. If it were up to me, I'd order takeout, although even that gets to be a pain because you have to get everyone to agree on the restaurant, not to mention that it costs a lot. Now that I'm in charge of ordering and paying, I'm realizing how it all adds up.

I'm wondering if I can get away with calling Dad for permission to put tonight's meal on the emergency credit card when the doorbell rings.

Scruffles barks but maintains his position by Mom's side.

"It's okay, Scruffs, go do your job," Mom tells him, giving him a gentle push with her hand.

He licks her hand and stays where he is, while I get up and head for the front hall.

I open the door and I'm floored when I see Rosa standing there, holding a bag of takeout from Mr. Nosh.

"Hey," she says, hesitating. "Mom and I . . . Well, we thought maybe you might want some dinner. You know, so you don't have to cook."

It's the first time she's said more than a curt hi to me in almost a month. Part of me wants to slam the door in her face for the way she's treated me.

At the same time, I've missed her like crazy.

I don't know what to say, but I open my mouth and out

tumbles: "You haven't spoken to me in weeks. Even when I texted you my mom had cancer." I take a deep breath to try to keep a grip on my anger. "Okay, so I did something wrong, but what kind of friend ignores texts like that? And now you're suddenly concerned about me not having to cook?"

Guess I was angrier than I thought.

A flush creeps over Rosa's cheeks and she looks down at the doormat. "I . . ." She looks up to meet my gaze. "Sammy, I know I haven't been the greatest friend lately—"

"Talk about an understatement," I say before she can finish. "I tell you my mom has *cancer* and you don't even answer my texts? Or call? You act like I don't even exist in school? I thought you were my best friend."

"I was *furious!*" Rosa explodes. "Can you blame me? After that stuff with your dad in the news and then what I read in your diary."

"I told you I was sorry about that!" I exclaim. "And I was. I mean, I am."

"I know, but then I find out that Margo's mom is also a racist and Margo lets her get away with it just to save her own skin—"

"And mine," I confess quietly. "Margo did it to save my skin, too."

Apparently, I've decided that brutal honesty is the best policy after what happened. Huh. Didn't expect that of myself.

"What?"

Rosa seems genuinely taken aback by this news, which surprises me, given that she obviously read my diary. But then I realize I hadn't written about my secret relief that Margo had done it so that Mrs. McHenry wouldn't call my parents. Seems there are some things even I'm too ashamed to put on paper.

"Margo's mom was going to call our parents to say we'd been drinking, even though we hadn't," I tell her. "And if she did, my parents would have found out that I'd gone to the concert." I let out a bitter chuckle. "They did anyway, because of the hack. But Margo thought she was covering for me."

"By selling me out," Rosa says. "So I'm the expendable friend."

"No!" I protest. "It's not like that. But . . . I can understand why you might feel that way. And I'm sorry."

"What about you, Sammy? We've been best friends forever, but you're writing about how bad I smell? Saying 'maybe it's a cultural thing.'" The pain I see in her eyes pierces me like a stiletto. "It's one thing to realize that Mrs. McHenry is a racist, but you? That was so messed up. I cried for hours after reading that."

I've felt bad a lot since the hack, but that's nothing compared to how awful I feel now, knowing how the words I wrote so carelessly hurt Rosa, even if she was never meant to see them. What was I even thinking by writing something like that? It's like if she wrote that I'm cheap or have a big nose, just because I'm Jewish.

"I'm really sorry, Rosa," I tell her. "It was a stupid, awful thing to write. I don't know what I was thinking. I know it's no excuse, but I wrote it at like, I don't know, five in the morning when I'd barely slept and I was in a really bad mood because we had to leave the concert early."

Rosa doesn't say anything. She's looking down at the ground. I don't know if I should continue, but I do.

"I was just venting. I never thought anyone would see it— especially not the entire world."

Rosa looks me straight in the eye. "But you still thought it," she says.

"Rosa, you know me. We've been best friends since elementary school. I'm not a racist. Really. I'm just an idiot. Don't years of actions speak louder than a few stupid words?"

Rosa shifts the Mr. Nosh bag from one hand to another. I get a whiff of Chinese food, and my traitorous stomach gives such a loud growl I'm sure she can hear it.

"I guess even nonracists can say stupid hurtful things," she said. "At least you didn't try to justify it by saying, 'I'm not racist! My best friend is Hispanic!'"

"Even if she is," I joke, hoping that she's ready to laugh about it.

Luckily, she is.

"You're such a dork," she says. "Since we're doing true confessions, the truth is, some of my crazier relatives still call Jews *asesinos de Cristo*. I tried arguing with them once, but it wasn't worth it. It just ruined the family gathering and didn't end up changing their minds."

She holds out the bag, a peace offering, hope in her brown eyes.

"Anyway, I know how you love Mr. Nosh. So I thought it might cheer you up."

Smiling, I take it. Good friends are worth forgiving. "You're right. I *do* love Mr. Nosh. So does RJ. He'll be psyched," I say. "Wanna stay?"

"I . . . Okay," Rosa says. "If you're sure your mom's up to it."

"She's a little out of it from the painkillers, but I'm sure a quick hello is fine," I tell her, gesturing for her to come inside.

Scruffles comes scampering over to say hi, wagging his tail and sniffing in the direction of the Mr. Nosh bag. The smell of food has clearly overcome his devotion to Mom.

"Hey, puppy, long time no see!" Rosa says. "Sorry, this isn't for you, buddy."

Scruffles follows us into the kitchen, looking hopeful nonetheless.

"Mom, Rosa's here," I call to my mother. "She brought us dinner."

"It's from my mom, too," Rosa says, going in to say hi to Mom. "She sends her love and said to call her if you need anything, no matter what."

"I will," Mom says. "And thanks for bringing dinner. It's been tough on Sammy, having to take over so much on top of school and, well, . . . everything that's been going on." She smiles at me. "But she's been incredible. I couldn't do this without her."

I wish we didn't have to do this at all. But since we have to, I'm glad that Mom feels like I'm being incredible. I don't feel all that incredible. Mostly, I feel scared and overwhelmed. It's pretty much all I can do to put one foot in front of the other and keep going.

"Are you hungry at all, Mom?" I ask. "I can make you a plate and bring it in here."

"No, I'm a little sleepy," she says. "You and RJ go ahead and eat whenever you're ready."

Her eyelids are already practically closed, and I know she'll probably be back asleep in five minutes.

Rosa takes a worried glance at Mom and follows me back into the kitchen. "Is she going to be okay?" she whispers.

"The sun will come out . . . tomorrow." I play that stupid song in my head. *Think Positive. Ninety-three is a much bigger number than seven. Most people would take that bet.*

"The prognosis is good," I reply quietly, but with more assurance than I actually feel. "She starts chemo in a few weeks, and that's the worst part, from what we've been told."

"That makes her lose her hair, right?" Rosa asks.

I nod, wondering how RJ is going to deal when that happens, even though Mom's warned us that it's coming.

"She's trying to make the best of it. She said she's always

wanted to try having crazy-colored hair. She's talking about getting a purple wig."

Rosa laughs. "No way! Your mom in a purple wig? That I'll have to see!"

"Well, you'll have to come here, because RJ and I made her promise not to wear it in public. We've got enough problems at school without being known for our Crazy Purple-Haired Cancer Mom."

As soon as I mention problems at school, Rosa stops laughing. She crosses her arms over her stomach, and her shoulders round inward, making her appear smaller than she already is.

"Sammy, I . . . I'm sorry again that I haven't been a good friend recently. And I couldn't have picked a worse time. I was just so . . . *mad*."

"I know, you had every right to be, and—"

"No, *I'm* sorry. Because you made a good point. We've all said stuff about each other behind our backs. You just got caught."

"I never meant to hurt you," I explain. "I was just venting. To myself. Or at least I thought it was to myself. I was just trying to get stuff out of my head so it didn't bother me as much."

Rosa twists the end of a lock of hair. "I get that now I've had more time to think about it." She glances away, then meets my gaze full on. "I messed up, too. I ditched my best friend when she needed me most because I was hurt and angry. And it took me this long to reach out to you to work it out."

She takes a deep breath as if to summon her courage, and says, "I'm really sorry for that. I've missed you, Sammy. You're my best friend. I hate us being mad at each other."

"Me too," I confess. "More than you can imagine."

We smile at each other shyly and then fall into a bear hug. Her hair tickles my nose, smelling of the shampoo she's used since sixth grade; the scent of familiarity, flowers, friendship.

Just then RJ comes into the kitchen. He does a double take, seeing Rosa and me hugging it out.

"So I take it you guys are friends again?" he asks, getting right to the point.

Rosa and I break apart, look at each other, and laugh.

"I guess you could say that," I tell him.

"Girls are weird," RJ observes. "One minute you guys are friends, then you're enemies, then you're friends again." He spots the takeout bag. "Hey, is that Mr. Nosh for dinner?"

"Yeah, it was my peace offering," Rosa says.

"Well, even if Sammy doesn't forgive you, I do," RJ says. "Can we eat? I'm starving!"

Scruffles thumps his tail against the cabinets in agreement.

"Me too," I say.

We spread out the takeout and feast on our favorite dishes from Mr. Nosh, which of course Rosa knows because best friends do. She even ordered RJ chicken fried rice, which he shares with Scruffles, though we're not supposed to give the dog human food. Whatever. It feels like a celebration, and we haven't had much reason to do that lately.

"So I'm not following the prom Instagram anymore," I confess. "Did you get a dress?"

"Yeah, I did," Rosa says. "It was weird to go shopping for it without you."

She takes out her cell and shows me a picture. The dress she bought is super cute—dark blue chiffon with pearls and sequin-beaded bodice. It's very Rosa—and of course she's bought crazy high heels to match, which I'd never be able even to walk in no matter how hard I tried.

"So does this mean you've totally given up on the idea of prom?" Rosa asks. "I'm sure I could find you a date if you want to go. Even if you just go as friends."

I hesitate, not sure if telling her about our alternative plans will seem like I'm being, I don't know. Hipster-wannabe? Hostile? A hostile hipster?

But we're best friends again. That means being honest.

"I've given up on real prom, yeah," I admit. "But a bunch of us have been planning a Faux Prom."

Rosa chokes on a mouthful of sesame noodles, and RJ has to pat her on the back. I go refill her glass of water while she recovers.

"Are you serious?" she asks, when she finally swallows and recovers her breath. "A *Faux Prom*?"

"Yeah. A low-key, low-expense party for the social pariahs who for one reason or another don't think they'd feel comfortable at prom."

"But . . . you could have a good time," Rosa argues. "You'll come in my group and—"

"Yeah, and you'll be off dancing with Eddy, and I'll be surrounded by the same people who have been talking about me and staring at me and making fun of me for the last few weeks. Sounds like my idea of a good time . . . not."

Rosa is quiet, staring down at her plate.

"Rosa, do you have any idea what it's been like at school?"

RJ has been concentrating on eating, just listening and helping himself to more chicken with cashews, but here he's got my back.

"It's the worst," he says. "And that's even without having my journal posted, because I'd never be dumb enough to write a journal."

"I'm sorry," Rosa says, her voice soft. "I want to go to prom and I want you to be there with me, the way we always pictured it. It's hard to imagine it any other way. I'm selfish, I guess."

"Not selfish—just my best friend," I assure her. "But life happens. Bad things surprise you when you least expect them. I've had to learn to deal with that. And I just can't go to prom with the way things are. Are you . . . okay with that?"

"I'm not okay with it. I hate it. But I have to accept that's the way it is." Rosa sighs. "I guess there's always senior prom, right?"

"Definitely," I agree, not that I can think that far ahead, with everything that's going on.

"Besides, she's grounded anyway," RJ points out. "She still hasn't earned back prom rights."

"I will!" I protest. "I just didn't want to bug Dick and Helene with asking about it yet. It's been so crazy around here."

"So who all's going to this Faux Prom?" Rosa asks. "And where is it?"

"It's at BethAnn Jackson's house," I tell her. "There's about thirty people coming so far."

"Are notorious outcasts allowed to have dates?" Rosa asks.

I motion to RJ with my eyes. Rosa catches the hint, but RJ, who heard the question, doesn't give up on finding out the answer.

"Well? Are they?" he asks.

Great. The last thing I want to do is talk about Noah in front of my brother.

But on the other hand, trying to keep my journal away from RJ was why I wrote it on my laptop, and that's how I got in so much trouble in the first place.

"Yes. They are allowed to have dates. And mine is Noah Woods."

Rosa's eyes widen. "Noah from SAT prep? Quiet, geeky Noah?"

That's probably what I would have said about him myself not that long ago. But now that I know him better, it seems so . . . *inadequate* to hear him described that way. Noah's so much more than that.

"Funny, smart Noah, who has been a killer friend when I really needed one," I say, with determination.

"*Oooh*. Sammy has a crush on Noah," RJ says, snickering. "*Sammy and Noah, sitting in a tree. K-I-S-S-I-N-G!*"

Example A of why the last thing I wanted to do is talk about my date in front of my brother.

"Don't you have some homework to do or something?" I ask, giving him a pointed *Get lost* look.

"I did it already," he says, smirking. "Besides, I haven't had my fortune cookie yet."

"Neither have I," Rosa says. "Come on, we all have to read ours aloud."

Picking the right cookie is a big deal for Rosa. She waves her hand over them until one sends out the "right energy." RJ grabs the nearest one and I do eeny meeny miny mo between the two leftover ones.

"'Land is always on the mind of a flying bird,'" RJ reads. "I don't even know what that means."

"It's obvious, grasshopper," I tell him. "If you don't have a home, you're always looking for one."

"Or not," Rosa says. "It could mean that even when you're flying high, you need to stay grounded."

"You guys have no idea what you're talking about," RJ says. "You're just making this stuff up as you go along."

Most of the time we're faking it. That's what Dad said. Maybe part of growing up is realizing that they're just like us, but older and maybe a bit wiser. Making stuff up as they go along, and pretending they know what they're doing.

"That's what you think," I say, pretending just like the best of them. "Go on, Rosa, read yours."

"'Time may fly by. But memories don't,'" she reads, wrinkling her brow. "That's . . . profound."

"I want to forget the memories of now," RJ says. "It's been a total MiseryFest."

My mouth opens to agree with him, but I don't say the words. Because I realize that even though RJ's right, it *has* been a total MiseryFest—I don't want to forget it, exactly. But I do want to be at a point in the future when I can look back at the pain and it's pixelated and fuzzy and doesn't hurt so much.

Maybe someday we can even look back on this time and laugh. But most of all, we'll know we got through it. We got dropped into this awful situation and kept going until we came out the other side. And we'll know that we can do it if something bad ever happens to us again.

"Come on, Sammy, stop catching flies and open yours," RJ says, feeding the last crumb of his cookie to Scruffles.

I open the cellophane, break apart my cookie, and extract the fortune. "'We cannot change the direction of the wind, but we can adjust our sails,'" I read.

Just then, as if on cue, Scruffles lets out an incredibly loud, stinktastic fart.

"Scruffles! Gross!" Rosa shrieks, jumping up and moving to the other side of the table.

Scruffles waves his tail along the floor, as if trying to sweep the scent in her direction.

"We cannot change the direction of the wind," I repeat, feeling a fit of giggling coming on.

RJ is pinching his nose with his fingers to block the smell.

"But we sure wish we could!" he exclaims in a nose-pinched nasal voice.

"What is going on in there?" Mom calls from the family room. "Sounds like I'm missing a party!"

"Sorry . . . did we wake you up?" I shout back, feeling guilty.

She shuffles in, looking a tiny bit less tired and pale than she had earlier. "It's okay. It's nice to hear you having a good time," Mom says. "What's so funny?"

"Scruffles farted," RJ says, his fingers still pinched over his nose. "Can't you smell?"

"*That's* what's causing all the hilarity?" Mom says, raising her hands to the ceiling and giving Rosa a look of mock despair. "The *dog passing gas*?"

Rosa nods. "Farts are funny. What can I say?"

"Well, as much as I'd like to pull a Queen Victoria and tell you 'We are not amused,' I have to agree, Rosa. They are," Mom admits. "I'm just glad the air cleared before I got here."

There's one fortune cookie left. I hand it to Mom. "Here. Your turn to read your fortune," I say.

Mom opens the wrapper and actually bites her cookie open, which means she must be feeling better. She slides the paper out of the remaining shell as she finishes chewing.

"'A light heart carries you through all the hard times,'" she reads. Surveying us all with a warm smile, Mom says, "Sounds like good advice to me. Got any good poop jokes?"

May 7

AP Stats tomorrow. LAST ONE. The probability that I will collapse into an exhausted stress heap tomorrow afternoon is 100 percent. Well, after I drive RJ home from Odyssey of the Mind, that is. I'm thinking of printing up a Sammy's Chauffeur Service sign for the car.

Kidding. It's not that bad. I'd much rather drive RJ than have to help Mom empty the drains. And RJ and I have had some interesting convos in the car. Maybe it's because we're not at home. Or maybe it's the enclosed space that feels safe. It's just us and whatever music we're playing and what's on our minds that day.

This afternoon when I picked him up from Photography Club, he showed me a picture he'd taken of Mom asleep on the sofa. Scruffles is curled up at her feet, his head resting on her leg. Her eyes are closed, but the dog is keeping watch with one eye open. RJ printed and matted the picture so it's ready for framing.

"Do you think Mom will like it, or do you think she's going to complain about how she looks asleep?" RJ asked me.

"Nobody looks good when they're asleep except for babies," I pointed out. "She'll love it."

He kept staring at the picture, the whole ride home.

"She's going to get better, right?" he asked just as we were pulling in the driveway.

257

I didn't know what to say. Tell him the probabilities? 93 percent should be reassuring, but RJ is my brother and he wakes up screaming from nightmares. I think there's a pretty high probability that he'd start worrying about the 7 percent, too. Tell him I have no idea, and until Mom finishes chemo nobody else does, either?

RJ's trying to be brave just like me, but he looked so scared in that moment that I decided to give him the comfort I wish I felt, even if it meant telling a white lie.

"Yeah. The chemo is going to make her feel worse for a while, but she's definitely going to get better."

It was worth it just to see the relief on his face, and the way he jumped out of the car and practically bounced into the house to give Mom the picture.

I sat in the garage after I pulled the car in, wondering if I did the right thing. I'd promised myself that I was going to be honest from now on. No more lies.

But like the fortune said, I've had to learn to adjust my sails of expectation to meet the changing winds. I won't pretend it's been easy. It's been a lot harder than the AP exams I spent so many hours studying for and stressing about. For as long as I can remember, everyone has been telling me how important doing well on those AP exams is for the Rest of My Life—my parents, teachers, and the administrators at school. But isn't learning how to cope when life derails your train from the tracks just as important?

I think it is. I know it is. Even if I never use AP Statistics again in my life, I know the probability of more bad things happening to me in the future is 100 percent—without even doing any calculations. It's not because I'm pessimistic. It's because that's just the way life is. Stuff happens, even when you are doing your best to think positively.

sixteen

After I finish my homework, I go down to the living room, where Mom is on the sofa attempting to do some work. Grandma is in the kitchen making dinner for us, and RJ came home on the bus, so I figure it's okay for me to take a tiny break from being Daughter of the Year.

"I'm just going over to Rosa's," I tell Mom. "I'll be back in an hour."

Mom looks up from her laptop, frowning. "Grandma's been here all day. She might need your help with dinner."

"Seriously?" I blurt out, surprised. "I finished APs yesterday and I've been Cinder-Sammy ever since I got my license and you're giving me a hard time about escaping to Rosa's for an hour?"

"Did you forget that you were grounded?"

"How could I? I've been trying really hard to be the

perfect daughter so I can earn back my privileges and go to prom."

"Giving me attitude isn't going to get you very far," Mom snaps.

"I'm not giving you attitude! I'm just trying to stay sane!" I shout.

"I really don't need this right now, Sammy," Mom says. "I've just had surgery and I'm trying to catch up on work."

"You think *I* need this right now? Do you think I need any of the stuff that's happened? Jeez, Mom, listen to yourself."

I'm so furious at her that I storm back up to my room, slamming the door and flinging myself on the bed to explode into an angry scream into my pillow. It's *so unfair*. I've been working my butt off at school and putting myself out to help at home. I've done things that freak the heck out of me because Mom needs my help. But nothing I do is ever enough. They always expect more.

After I scream myself out, though, guilt seeps in. I'd vowed to be nicer to Mom, and I just yelled at her for having cancer. Who does that?

But I can't help it. There's too much to deal with while trying to hold it all together and be perfect. If I stay grounded, if Mom and Dad don't let me go to Faux Prom, I'm afraid I'll lose it. It's probably not the best time to talk to them after I've just had this blowup with Mom, but I need to know

I have this to look forward to. Definitely. Positively. Not maybe, if I hit some ever-raising bar.

There's a knock on my door.

"Sammy? It's Grandma. Can I come in?"

"Okay," I say, sitting up and fixing my mess of hair.

Grandma Sally opens the door and comes in, taking a seat on the end of my bed. She pats my leg comfortingly.

"It's been tough for you, I know."

"At least *someone* does."

Grandma sighs. "Your parents do, too, Sammy, even though it might not seem that way."

"It definitely doesn't seem that way. Not at all. They just expect me to slay it in school and help around the house and be perfect in every single way. And the one time I mess up, it's like I'm the Demon Child from the Planet Fail."

Grandma laughs. "You do have an amusing way of putting things, dear."

"Mom and Dad don't find it amusing. They call it attitude and they don't have time for it."

"Sweetie, they're overwhelmed with their own problems and anxieties right now. It's making it hard for them to see the big picture."

"But they're my *parents*," I complain, sitting up and leaning forward, legs crossed, to make my point better. "They always tell me my job is doing well in school. Parenting is supposed to be *their* job."

"Yes, but nobody's perfect. Going through especially stress-ful times can bring out the best in people, but it can also sometimes reveal . . . their less attractive traits."

I think about how Margo was so quick to throw away our friendship.

"Yeah, I know what you mean." I sigh.

"Your mom and dad love you so much, Sammy," Grandma says. "And so do Grandpa and I. We're all going to get through this."

"But, Grandma, I need a break . . ." I have to stop and blot my eyes. "It's all too much. I need a light at the end of the tunnel, something to look forward to."

"I know. When your father gets home tonight, talk to your parents again. Be calm. Be polite. But tell them how you feel."

"They won't listen. You heard Mom just now. She wasn't listening."

"Keep trying," Grandma urges me. "You'll be surprised what actually sinks in."

She gets up and kisses me on the forehead. "Dinner's all ready to go. I spoke to your dad and he promises that he's on the way home and will be here in half an hour. All you have to do is turn on the oven to three fifty and heat it up," she says. "I've already set the table."

"Sorry, Grandma," I say, feeling guilty all over again. "RJ and I have been taking turns doing that. Tonight was my night."

"I know. I saw the chart on the refrigerator," she says. "But it was obvious you needed a night off."

I lean forward and hug her. "Thanks, Grandma," I say.

"You don't have to thank me," she tells me. "Just take care of yourself."

"If it's so obvious to you I need a night off, why doesn't Mom get it?" I ask.

Grandma looks down at her hands, twisting the wedding rings on her finger. "Sometimes mothers don't see their teenage daughters clearly," she says. And looking me in the eye, she says, "But the same goes for teenage daughters and their mothers."

I open my mouth to argue, but she doesn't give me a chance.

"Listen to me, Sammy. Age might give me aching bones and liver spots, but it's also taught me a thing or two," Grandma says. "Your mother loves you, just like you love her." She stands up and strokes the hair back from my forehead. "Now tonight, when your father gets home, I want you to sit down with your parents and have a conversation about going to the prom. Tell them what you told me."

"They won't listen."

"Try them," Grandma says. "Maybe you'll be surprised."

Surprised is definitely what I will be, but I promise her that I'll attempt the conversation before she kisses me and leaves to go home.

Dad gets home in time for dinner. Grandma made us a roast chicken with mashed potatoes and green beans. She'd already carved the chicken and made a gravy from the pan drippings, so all I have to do is heat everything up. It's the best dinner we've had since the last time Grandma cooked for us. Takeout and whatever I've been cobbling together for dinner is no competition for Grandma's cooking.

"It looks like I might have to go down to Washington next week," Dad says. "I'm being called to testify before the House Financial Services Committee."

Mom's fork clatters to her plate. "You have to travel? Now?"

"It would just be overnight," Dad says. "I still have a bank to run."

"I know," she says. "But I wish you didn't have to go."

"I wish I didn't, either," Dad says.

"Can't you tell them that Mom's sick?" RJ asks.

"I'm the chief executive officer of the bank, RJ. When things go wrong, people look to me to find out why."

RJ pushes his string beans, which he's been trying to avoid eating, around his plate with his fork. "But why can't it wait?" he asks. "Till Mom's better?"

"'Cause that's not the way the world works," I tell him. "You can't tell Congress to wait."

"Why not?" RJ says. "It's not like they do anything on time. They always vote on the budget at the eleventh hour."

Mom and Dad stare at RJ and then look at each other and burst out laughing.

"What?" he asks. "What's so funny?"

"Your eighth-grade political punditry," Dad says.

"It's so on target," Mom agrees.

RJ looks confused, but I give him a look like *See, they do think you're smart,* and he glows in the light of their approval.

Just like I do, I guess. But I'm exhausted from the struggle of trying to get it.

Still, I promised Grandma that I'd try, even though the thought of it makes me feel like Sisyphus and the boulder will just roll back down the hill.

"Mom, Dad . . . Can I talk to you about prom?" I ask. "It's only two and a half weeks away, and I want to know if I can go. I've been working really hard, I've been responsible, and I think I've earned it."

I have to swallow the lump that rises in my throat, because Grandma told me to be "calm and polite" and I'm pretty sure by that she meant "don't cry."

"Besides," I continue, "it's been hard with exams and how things have been at school because of the hack, and now Mom's cancer. It would really help to have something fun to look forward to. Especially since I still have to study for the SAT and Mom's going to start chemo in two weeks."

Mom looks down at her half-eaten meal and doesn't say anything. The lump in my throat feels like it's going to choke off my breathing. If they say no, I don't know how I'll go on.

"Please," I say to Dad, since at least he's still giving me eye contact. "I need this."

Dad looks over at Mom and my heart contracts.

Don't shut me down. Please.

"Helene? What do you say?" he asks her. "I think Sammy's earned back the right to go, don't you?"

No. Words. For. What. Feels. Like. Hours.

Till finally Mom raises her head and says, "Yes, Dick. I think she has."

I can't believe it.

"For real? I can go?"

Dad smiles. "Yes, Cinderella, you can go to the ball."

"Sammy's got a date already," RJ reveals. "His name's Noah. He's her *boyfriend*."

My father raises an eyebrow. "Boyfriend, huh? That's news to Dear Old Dad."

"And to Dear Not-So-Old Mom," Mom adds. "Not Ice-Cream Parlor Boy, I hope."

"No way!" I exclaim. I glare at RJ. "And Noah's not my boyfriend."

Yet, at least. We're friends, who like each other a lot. I think he's cute and funny and thoughtful. But I've been too busy with exams and Mom's cancer and being grounded to think about putting a name on what we are. But my heart beats a little faster thinking about it.

"Can I take you dress shopping before I start chemo?" Mom asks.

"Definitely! Well . . . as long as you don't mind going to Goodwill," I tell her.

Dad almost chokes on a forkful of mashed potatoes. "Goodwill?" he sputters. "Sheesh, Sammy, things aren't that bad. I'm still employed. I can afford to buy you a prom dress."

"*We* can afford," Mom says, laying down her fork like a gauntlet. "I work, too, in case that slipped your mind, dear."

Dad throws her a sheepish look. "We can still afford to buy you a prom dress," he corrects himself.

"It's not that, Dad," I say. "It's because I'm going to Faux Prom and—"

"What on earth is a Faux Prom?" Dad asks.

He doesn't sound amused by the idea. I hope this doesn't change his mind about letting me go.

"It's just that since the hack, things have been really awful at school," I confess, finally telling them just how bad things have been. "Margo completely ditched me. She doesn't even talk to me anymore. In fact, she trash-talks me to anyone who will listen. Even Rosa didn't even talk to me for a while, but we've made up now."

Dad opens his mouth to speak and then closes it. I don't know if he's really hearing, but since he's still listening, I go on.

"This girl BethAnn—the one who got tormented online because she said no after being pressured into saying yes to a fancy promposal—well, she was actually nice to me because of what I'd written in my journal about her. She knew I understood. And *she* understood how *I* felt. And . . . well, neither of us felt like going to prom with the same kids who have been jerks to us, so we decided to throw an alternative prom instead. Her parents agreed to host it at their house and they'll totally be home and I really, really want to go there instead." I take a deep breath. "And that's Faux Prom."

My father is now the one staring at his dinner plate like his half-eaten chicken leg holds the clues to the secrets of the universe.

"But, Sammy, what does that have to do with buying a prom dress at Goodwill?" Mom asks, picking up the slack.

"Oh. Because we decided to make it the anti-prom. Prom is so out of hand. The promposals. The dresses and tuxes. The limos. The corsages—I mean, what's even the point of those?"

"Tradition, I guess," Mom says. "Besides, flowers are pretty."

"Tradition! Tradition!" RJ pipes up, singing the song from *Fiddler on the Roof.*

"Thanks for the musical interlude, weirdo," I tell him. "I know flowers are pretty, Mom, but I don't need to wear them on my wrist."

Mom nods. "Okay, if this is what you're doing, I'll take you to Goodwill."

And the strange thing is, I find myself looking forward to it.

May 10

Rosa came to Goodwill with Mom and me to help find a dress for Faux Prom. Besides dressing from Goodwill, everyone has to bring some cans or dry goods for the food bank.

"That's a cool idea," Rosa said. "Why don't we do it at Real Prom?"

I didn't have a good answer. Maybe because everyone's so busy worrying about creating and/or getting the most viral promposal, and then getting the most photogenic dress/tux combo and then renting a limo and getting invited to the right after-parties that the food bank isn't exactly on their minds?

Even though Rosa already bought her prom dress, she still tried on some of the retro offerings with me at Goodwill. We had a blast. I ended up getting a sixties scoop-neck sheath, in shocking pink. Mom said it made me look like Audrey Hepburn. I laughed and said, "Yeah, if Audrey Hepburn were Jewish and had curly hair and curves."

It helps so much to have something fun to look forward to, even if it wasn't what I'd originally hoped for. In some ways, though, it's turning out to be better. It's like getting on a train thinking you're going to one place that you really wanted to go, but ending up at a different destination that turns out to be even more interesting.

Mom starts chemo in eleven days. We went out wig shopping and she bought two wigs, one in her usual color and one in purple, just like she promised. After Goodwill, we stopped at the pharmacy and I bought her some Glittery Grape nail polish to match her wig. That night, I did Mom's nails for her and she put on the wig and she said she was going to be the funkiest mom in the carpool line.

RJ immediately reminded her that she's promised not to wear the purple wig in public, but I think it suits her, so I said she should totally break that rule. RJ eventually gave in, after I got him alone and gave him my Grandpa Marty "It's better than the alternative" imitation. It's amazing how that puts things in perspective.

Ever since the fart joke incident, we've been trying to keep the humor level high, since it seemed to do Mom so much good.

RJ and I got together in his room last week and between us we subscribed to thirty different "Joke a Day" email lists, so we always have a supply of silly humor on hand. BethAnn suggested I start a Tumblr, so I did—Humor for Healing. When I told Grandma Sally and Grandpa Marty about it, Grandpa emailed me Proverbs 17:22: "A cheerful heart brings good healing, but a crushed spirit dries up the bones."

It's not been easy to keep a happy heart with everything that's going on.

I've had to learn how to get through every single painful moment when my spirit does feel broken, when I'm overwhelmed with sadness or anxiety or anger or guilt, or sometimes all of them in one giant tornado of feeling so that it feels like I'm going to *explode from the pressure. Sometimes it feels just too hard for one person. Sometimes it is. Writing in a diary helps, but it's not enough. You need people. People who listen, who understand because they've been through what you have, or who do their best to even though they haven't. And sometimes, you just need to be around people who know when to tell a good fart joke.*

SeVeNTeeN

Even though we've been warned that chemo is going to make Mom tired and probably sick, it's not until she starts the first round that we truly understand just *how* tired and sick. Grandma Sally took her to the hospital because Dad had to go to work—the repercussions of the hack are still ongoing and now he has to testify before another congressional committee, this time the Senate Committee on Banking, Housing, and Urban Affairs. When I get home from school, Mom is in bed.

"How is she?" I ask Grandma.

"Wiped out," Grandma says. "Completely. She barely has the energy to get herself out of bed to go to the bathroom."

"Is it okay to visit her?"

"Sure, honey," Grandma says. "But if she's sleeping, let her rest."

The curtains are closed in my parents' bedroom, leaving the light dim. I can barely see the outline of my mother's form in the king-size bed.

Tiptoeing to the side of the bed, I listen for her breath, relieved when I hear her exhale.

I go to the other side of the bed and crawl in next to her, not wanting to wake her up by holding her hand. Instead, I clutch the bottom of her T-shirt between my fingers and lie beside my mom, listening to her breathing.

"Don't stop, Mom," I whisper. "Just keep going. We're going to get through this together."

I want her to wake up. I need her to wake up to show me she's going to survive this. But Grandma says Mom needs rest.

Gently squeezing her hand with its Glittery Grape painted nails, I get off the bed and leave Mom to sleep, closing the door behind me.

When Mom does wake up, she's still feeling rough. We have to make sure she drinks lots of fluids to flush the drugs through her system, but she doesn't want to drink or eat.

"I can't, Mom, I feel too nauseous," she complains when Grandma Sally tries to get her to take sips from a glass of water through a straw.

"Just a few more sips," Grandma cajoles her. "We have to keep up your fluids."

Mom reluctantly gives in to Grandma's nagging, but as soon as she's taken a few sips, she gestures for the bucket, which we've been keeping by the side of the bed in case she feels sick.

The moment I give it to her, she heaves, but there's not much in her stomach to throw up.

Grandma strokes Mom's hair away from her face.

"My poor baby," she says. "This isn't any fun."

"Understatement of the year," Mom groans into the bucket.

It's weird to watch my mom being taken care of by Grandma. As Grandma wipes Mom's face with a cool washcloth and then straightens the sheets around her, I see my own mom's gestures when she's looked after a sick me. Mom clings to Grandma's hand tightly as if there's magic there that will help her to feel better, just as I did to Mom when I was little. I wish like anything I could give that comfort and strength back to her now.

I leave Grandma with Mom and go downstairs to make dinner for the rest of us. I guess when you're feeling awful, it doesn't matter how old you are. You still want your mom.

Dad comes home relatively early, considering everything that's on his plate at work. He talks privately with Grandma to catch up on what's been happening here, then heads upstairs to see Mom as soon as Grandma leaves.

I give Dad some time with Mom alone, but then I go up to see if there's anything my mother wants or needs.

"I'm fine, honey," Mom says.

"Sally said you need to try to drink more fluids," Dad tells her. "How about sipping a little ginger ale?"

"Ugh, no," Mom groans. "Just the thought . . . bleah."

"How about if I cut up some watermelon?" I suggest. "You could try eating a few little pieces."

I'd read about watermelon on an online chemotherapy support board—people who actually were going through chemo and trying to figure out how to stay hydrated when they felt sick and their taste buds were messed up from the chemicals comparing notes on different suggestions with each other.

To my surprise, Mom says, "Watermelon. That sounds good."

I practically run down to the kitchen, I'm so excited that there's something my mother wants to eat. I slice the watermelon into thin pieces, so it will virtually melt on her tongue, and then bring the plate upstairs. Dad is on the bed next to Mom, holding her cradled against his chest. He takes the plate from me and gently holds a piece of fruit to her lips.

"Here you go, Hels," he says. "Try this."

I stand next to the bed, with the bucket to hand, just in case. But Mom swallows, takes a breath, and smiles.

"Great idea, Sammy," she says. "I could go for another."

"Your wish is my command," Dad says, feeding her some more watermelon.

As I watch Dad sitting with my mom, taking amazing care of her, I wonder how he can be one way at home with us, and then stand by while people say the kind of things they did in those emails about his colleague Aisha Rana. How do I reconcile that?

I'm not going to be able to trust him again, or trust anyone totally, until I've found the answer to that question—and the only way I'm going to do that is to ask again.

I know he's tired and stressed and worried. I know it's probably not the best time to ask. But I don't know if there will ever be a right time to have this conversation.

I wait till he's gone downstairs. I thought he'd be in his study working on the testimony for the congressional hearing, but he's slumped on the sofa in the family room in front of the TV with a beer. Comedy Central is blaring out of the TV, instead of the news or the History Channel, which are usually the only channels Dad watches.

I turn to go upstairs, to leave him to relax in peace. But then I stop. I'm under stress, too. And because my parents haven't been honest with me—because they haven't told me the things I need to know under the vague illusion of protecting me, they made it way worse. And while they expect so much of me in school, they didn't think I could actually deal with the real world.

"Dad, we need to talk," I say.

I wonder if my words make his heart sink the same way it does when my parents tell me we have to talk. I wonder if he thinks, *Uh-oh, this can't be good.*

Dad looks like he's coming out of a trance. "What's that, kiddo?"

"Can I talk to you about something?"

"Sure," he says, switching off the TV, but I can't help noticing the sigh as he does it. He was switching off, and I'm making him switch on again.

I start to feel guilty, but too bad. Being my dad is his job, too.

He pats the sofa next to him, but I take a seat on the chair opposite, where Mom sat when she confronted me about going to the concert. I want to look him in the eye when we talk. We've been not talking about this for long enough and I don't want to have him put his arm around me and give me comfort and say, "It's okay," and believe it when it's not, just because he's my dad.

"What's on your mind?"

"The emails. The ones the hackers posted."

Dad's brow wrinkles in confusion. "They posted thousands of emails, Sammy. Could you be a little more specific?"

"The ones where you talk about Aisha Rana."

"Those again." My dad looks down at his beer bottle and starts picking at the label. "What is it you want to know?"

I want to know which is the real you.

But I can't ask him that. And even if I did, I'm not sure I'd trust the answer. What question can I ask that will give me a truthful answer?

"Yeah, Dad. *Those* again. The ones you avoid talking about every time I bring them up. I guess what I want to know is— no, forget that, I *need* to know—is that what I have to look forward to?"

"What do you mean?" he asks, still not looking at me.

"I *mean*, you always tell me I can do anything I want with my life if I work hard and do well in school. And I'm doing that despite everything raining down on my head, everything I thought was private about myself being made public through no fault of my own—"

"It wasn't my fault, either, Sammy."

"Well, it was even less my fault, Dad. You're at least the guy in charge at the bank. You at least had some control of the security. People reported to you on it, didn't they? You could have spent more money to upgrade the systems or trained people better or whatever. There's not a single thing *I* could have done to change the outcome of that except not keep a journal on my laptop."

"But—"

"Can you just listen to me instead of telling me the hack wasn't your fault!" I yell at him. "The hack isn't the point!"

My father sighs wearily. "So what is the point, Samantha?"

He's using my full name. That means he's getting impatient before I've even got out what I want to say. Too bad. I've waited long enough for this conversation to happen.

"You want the point, Dad? Fine. What I'm asking is, if I do all the things I'm supposed to do, all the things I'm doing now, and I get into a good college and then work hard there to get good grades so I can get a good job, is it just so I can get paid less than a guy and so someone else's dad will make comments about me like your colleagues did about Aisha Rana and then the head of my company won't do anything about it?"

My father finally looks up from his beer-label picking, stricken, like I've gut-punched him. Good, because that's exactly how I felt when I read those emails.

Now will he show me who the real Dick Wallach is?

He puts the beer bottle down on the table and buries his face in his hands. His breathing is loud and heavy, and I don't know if he's trying to control his temper or fighting back other emotions he doesn't want me to see.

Either way, my hands are trembling on my knees as the moments tick by, heavy with the weight of my unanswered question.

When he finally raises his head, he looks even more sad and weary than when I first walked into the room.

I did this to him.

No. I didn't. I just asked a question, one it was fair to ask. It's like he's never put two and two together to come up with the answer that a woman like Aisha Rana could be me some-day. When you think about it, that's pretty dumb for someone who is supposed to be as smart as my dad.

"I'm sorry, Sammy," he says. "I told you we just make it up as we go along. And that's not just with parenting."

That's his excuse?

"What do you mean? You're the head of the company. You've been on the cover of *Forbes* and *Fortune* and written up on *Bloomberg* and *Business Insider*. And you're just making it up as you go along?"

"Not when it comes to strategy. Business I know. Give me data, give me probabilities, give me facts and figures, I can deal with that. It's dealing with *people* where I have to make it up as I go along," Dad says. "Every time I think I've got the people thing figured out, another person comes along and changes the model."

Oh my god. Is he for real?

"Um . . . Dad . . . that's because people aren't widgets. They might share some common attributes, but they have infinite variables."

He sighs and gives me a tired, lopsided grin, which almost reminds me of Scruffles. "It's times like this when I wonder how my kids got to be so much smarter than me," he says.

"That's because we got the benefit of Mom's genes, too," I tell him. "Which brings me back to my question—which you still haven't answered. How can you tell me that I can do anything with my life, and then be okay with people writing stuff like that about a woman who works for you? How can you justify paying women less for doing the same job? Is that what I have to look forward to?"

Again, silence. Why won't he answer me? Is it because he can't?

I get up to leave, fighting off frustration. I don't want to believe that my dad is the Richard Wallach in those hacked emails, but if he can't even give me a straight answer, then maybe that's who he really is.

"Sammy, wait. Sit down."

I turn back, but I don't sit. I'm not in the mood to be ordered around like Scruffles.

"Please," Dad says.

I shake my head no and remain standing, arms crossed over my chest. My father sighs, and continues.

"We all play different roles in our lives, Sammy. I'm sure you do, too. You're a daughter when you're at home, and you're a student at school, and a friend when you're with your friends, and a babysitter when you babysit, and an employee when you have a summer job . . ."

"Okay, Dad, I get it. So?" I mean, Rosa and I talked about the same thing. I guess I just didn't get that while I was being different versions of myself, so is everyone else.

"So when I'm at home, I'm a husband and a father," Dad says. "And when I'm at work, I'm the CEO. And I have to play by the rules of that game, whether I happen to like those rules or not. Just like you might behave one way with one group of friends and another way with another."

"So you're saying you do it because everyone else does it?" I say. "Because that's completely lame, Dad. I can just imagine how you and Mom would react if I told you that's why I lied about going to the Einstein's Encounter concert." I put on my Dad imitation voice: "If all your friends jump off a cliff, are you going to do that, too?"

"I'm not saying it's because everyone else does it," Dad says. "Not exactly. It's that trying to change corporate culture is like trying to steer a supertanker. It takes a long time to change course. "

"But it's never going to change course if you keep doing the same thing," I point out. "You're the captain of the ship. The crew takes cues from you."

"I'm not the only captain. I'm just one captain of one ship," Dad says. "This is bigger than just me."

"You always quote Winston Churchill to me. Didn't he say 'I never worry about action, but only about inaction'? How are things going to get better for me and other girls like me, if my own dad as head of a company doesn't even try— if he just shrugs and says, 'That's the way things are in business'?"

By the time I'm done, I'm shaking with self-righteous anger. I just want to make him *see*. He has to understand. Why can't he get it? He's my *dad*. Doesn't he love me and want what's best for me?

Dad sinks his face in his hands again. He can't even stand to look at me. But then I hear a sound like the cry of a dying walrus. My dad's shoulders are shaking and I realize that he's crying.

Not just crying. My dad is sobbing.

All because of me. Okay, maybe not *exactly* because of me—he got himself here. But having to explain what he did to me was definitely a waterworks trigger in this moment.

But as mad as I am, I love my dad. And I've never seen him like this. So while I want nothing more than to keep yelling at him, I can't bring myself to. Because I think I need to be the bigger person. Which kind of sucks in terms of dealing with my frustration.

I move next to him on the sofa and put my arm around him and lay my head on his shoulder.

"It's okay, Dad. We'll be okay." At least I hope we will.

He raises his head, his eyes red, cheeks damp. I've never seen my dad show this much emotion before. He's always been the master of control.

"You've never reminded me as much of your mother as you did just now, Sammy," he says. "She makes me a better person. I can't lose her."

"You won't," I say. "We won't. We're going to fight this together. All of us."

Dad takes my hand.

"We will," he promises. "And I will fight for you, Sammy. Because you're right. I can't just make excuses when I'm the captain of the ship. Someone has to start giving the orders to change the course, and if it's not me, then who?"

I think I can believe him. I want to. This is the dad I've always thought I've known and loved.

Love is enough to make me give him the benefit of the doubt. Unless he proves me wrong.

May 24

It's almost here! Tomorrow night's prom—or for some of us, Faux Prom. Why couldn't they have scheduled prom the week AFTER the SAT instead of the week BEFORE? Then I wouldn't be sitting at home the night before prom, taking practice tests.

There are plenty of people who aren't at home doing that, judging from the pictures I'm seeing on Instagram. Maybe I wouldn't be either if Mom wasn't sick. If the hack hadn't happened, and I were going to the actual prom, I'd probably be getting together with Margo and Rosa and figuring out how we were going to do our hair and stuff like that.

Rosa told me she's going to get her hair done professionally in an updo tomorrow. If I had straight hair, I'd try to do an Audrey Hepburn updo to go with my dress, but with my mop o' frizz I'm not sure it'll work. I'm just going to pile it on my head, stick it with pins, and hope for the best.

Mom is still really tired and feeling sick, but she said today was a little bit better than yesterday and she hopes tomorrow will be better than today. The worst is knowing she has to go through another round in three weeks, and another round three weeks after that. Apparently the effects are cumulative—so she's going to feel worse each time. Ugh.

Mom says she just has to take it one day at a time and appreciate each little victory, like being able to enjoy watermelon.

"It gives you a real appreciation for the simple pleasures," she says. "Like being able to taste your food properly."

My appreciation of simple pleasures will be to have life back to normal again.

Ha! Normal. I've almost forgotten what a normal life feels like. Maybe abnormal is the new normal.

I do know this—life can never go back to how it was before the hack. Too much has changed. Friendships have changed. I've changed.

I was talking about this with Dad last night, and surprise, surprise, he had another Churchill quote to share: "There is nothing wrong in change, if it is in the right direction. To improve is to change, so to be perfect is to have changed often."

I've decided if I had a time machine and could go back and meet anyone in history, I'd want to go back and meet Winston Churchill. The guy seems to have had said something for every single situation that comes up in life. He was like a one-man quote machine. How did he do it? Did he just walk around uttering these profound things all the time? He'd be so awesome on Instagram or Tumblr.

I wonder if he ever wrote embarrassing things in his diary? Luckily for him, they only post the smart things he said online, not the dumb things.

But Churchill didn't get everything right, either. Just ask anyone in Australia or New Zealand about Gallipoli. Noah and I are going to watch that movie together once SAT is over. He said it was an antiwar war movie and I shouldn't miss it.

Everyone's got some kind of problem to get through. The important thing is to get up, keep going, and come out the other side.

eiGHTeeN

Grandma Sally insists on taking me for a manicure the morning of Faux Prom, even though I tell her it's not necessary.

"It's necessary for me," she says. "I had to wait a long time for grandchildren to spoil. Allow me to make the most of it."

"It would be ungrateful of me to deny you spoiling rights, Grandma," I say. "Go ahead. Do your worst. I mean, best. Spoil me to the end of the universe and back."

"How about just to the moon and back?" Mom says. "I still have to parent this child."

"Don't worry, Helene. I'll keep her civilized," Grandma assures Mom. "You've got enough on your plate."

Mom lifts her iced green tea in a mock toast. "I've actually kept a few things down from my plate today, so *L'Chaim.*"

L'Chaim. To Life.

I'll drink to that. Well, orange juice, at least.

Pampered Nails is already crowded when we get there, which isn't a surprise, considering it's junior prom tonight.

"We probably should have made a reservation." I sigh. "It's not usually this crazy, but with prom . . ."

"Don't worry. I'm in no rush. Go pick your color and I'll find out how long we have to wait."

There are so many girls around the polish shelves, I have to wait my turn to look.

"I thought you weren't going to prom."

It's Margo. She's there with Madison Maguire.

It's also the first time she's spoken to me directly since the day we fought after my journal was included in the data dump.

"What do you care? It's not like you've done anything except bad-mouth me for the last month," I say. "But as it happens, I'm not. I've got other plans."

I don't tell her what they are, and I think she's about to ask, but then she closes her lips and shrugs.

"That's too bad," Margo says. "I know how much you were looking forward to it."

Madison laughs. "The whole school knows that."

"Actually, the whole world knows it, if you're looking for accuracy in reporting, which clearly you aren't," I say. "But FYI, I'm looking forward to what I'm doing more." As the words come out of my mouth, I feel their truth, and it makes me throw back my shoulders and smile.

"Have fun tonight," I tell Margo, and without bothering to pick a color, I go over to Grandma Sally, who's still waiting in line to give the owner our names.

"It's okay, I can do my own nails," I tell her. "Let's just go to the drugstore and pick a color and then get some iced coffee."

"Are you sure, dear?"

"One hundred percent sure," I say. I don't need a probability tree to figure that out.

We go to the drugstore, and Grandma helps me pick the perfect shade of shocking pink to match my dress.

"Who makes up these names?" she laughs. "Flame War Flamingo?"

"How about this one?" I say, giggling as I hold up a different shade. "Too Darn Hot Pink?"

We amuse ourselves trying to see who can find the most ridiculous nail polish name. But the color we get to match my dress is perfect: Back to the Fuchsia.

On the way home in the car, Grandma Sally compliments me on my careful driving.

"You're kidding, right?"

"No, dear, I'm not. You drive very well," Grandma says. "It's a privilege for me to be chauffeured around by my granddaughter."

"It's easier to drive someone who isn't clutching the door handle and criticizing me every thirty seconds," I say.

"You're talking about your mother, I presume," Grandma says, giving me a shrewd sideways glance.

I plead the Fifth.

"You don't have to tell me, Sammy, because I did exactly the same thing to her, and she hated it just as much as you do and swore she would never do that to *her* kids," Grandma Sally tells me. "Which has made these last few years so . . . *interesting* . . . for me to watch."

I can't believe what I'm hearing. Mom's been better about the door clutching and criticism recently—I think she feels so awful after chemo that she barely notices my driving. But still.

"Are you telling me Mom's a hypocrite?"

Grandma sighs. "Darling, why go for hyperbole? I'm merely pointing out the cycle of life. Someday, God willing, you'll be lucky enough to have a smart, wonderful daughter, and I'll put money on the fact that you'll be in the passenger seat clutching the passenger door, just like your mother did to you."

No way! I promise my hypothetical future daughter. I will not do that to you. I will never be that annoying.

"By the time I have a kid learning to drive, they're going to have self-driving cars," I tell Grandma. "So I won't have to worry about that."

"Self-driving cars? *Oy gevalt*," she mutters, shaking her head in disapproval. "Computers are a wonderful invention, but they can never replace the human brain. It's like putting your trust in a golem."

"You mean the clay man that the rabbi in Prague made come to life by magic?"

"Yes, and guess what happened? The golem ran amok. These things never end well. The rabbi who created the golem had to destroy him," Grandma says. "Wait till your computerized car decides it has a mind of its own. Imagine asking . . . what's her name, Siri . . . to do something for you one day and only to have her reply, 'I'm sorry, Sammy, I can't do that.'"

"Don't take this the wrong away, Grandma, but maybe you're scared of technology because you're older," I say. "I've grown up with it, so it's second nature. My generation is more comfortable with it."

In the silence that follows, I wonder if I've gone too far.

"Tell me, my dear . . . how comfortable with technology were you when your journal was posted for the entire world to see?"

Ouch.

I never figured my *grandmother* would hit below the belt.

"Not at all," I admit. "But it was people doing the hacking. Humans are the weakest link."

"That's where we have a fundamental difference of opinion," Grandma Sally says. "Because while it's true that we all have our frailties and weaknesses, I don't believe a silicon chip and software can ever re-create the genius and creativity of the human spirit."

"I hope you're right, Grandma. Because if you're not, then eventually, there's not going to be much point to us, is there?"

I pull the car into the garage and turn off the engine. When I go to open the door, Grandma puts her hand on my arm to keep me in the car.

"Before we go in, I just want to say how proud I am of you for how much you've grown in the last couple of months. You've had a lot thrown at you, but you've managed to cope and still been a great help to your mom and dad," she says. "You should go out and have a magical evening tonight. You deserve it."

She fumbles in her handbag and takes out a small black silk pouch and hands it to me. "I want you to have these. Wear them in good health."

I open the pouch, and a single strand of luminous pearls falls into my lap. "Oh my god, they're so beautiful, Grandma," I exclaim, picking them up and fastening them around my neck so I can look at my reflection in the rearview mirror. "Thank you! They'll go perfectly with my dress."

"That's what I thought when you texted me a picture of the dress," Grandma says. "Those belonged to Great-Grandma Susan. I see so much of her in you: her spirit, her sense of humor, and her strength. She would be happy to know that her smart, loving, beautiful great-granddaughter is going to wear them now."

Throwing my arms around my grandmother's neck, I kiss her wrinkled cheek and breathe in the Chanel scent she wears.

"I love you, Sammy," she whispers.

"I love you, too, Grandma," I whisper back, a lump forming in my throat.

"You better go do your nails," Grandma says in a brisk and cheerful voice. "I understand this is some kind of Faux Prom for social pariahs, but you still should be a *well-groomed* pariah."

Laughter washes the lump away, and we go into the house so I can start getting ready.

At six, when I finally come downstairs all dressed and ready, there's a crowd waiting in the family room: Grandpa Marty, Grandma Sally, Mom, Dad, and RJ.

"See that gorgeous girl?" Grandpa Marty says, beaming with pride. "That's my granddaughter."

"Don't hog all the credit, Marty. She's *my* granddaughter, too," Grandma Sally says, smiling at me.

"I can't believe *my daughter* looks so grown up," Dad says.

"Ahem. I'd like to remind you all that I had quite a bit to do with the creation of this beautiful young lady," Mom says from the sofa.

"Ew! Mom, can you *not*?!" I exclaim.

Mom and Grandma exchange a glance and start laughing.

"What goes around comes around, Helene." Grandma chuckles.

"So what do you think, RJ?" I ask my brother, who is safe to ask because at least he can't make any claims about his part in my creation.

RJ looks up from his phone. "Yeah, you look nice."

"Just nice?"

"Really nice."

Hopefully, Noah will appreciate the effort a bit more. Like a lot more.

The doorbell rings ten minutes later, and I order everyone to stay where they are so Noah and I can get our first glimpse of each other dressed up without the embarrassment of a family audience. Scruffles is the only one who is exempt, because I can trust him not to embarrass me.

Famous last words . . .

As soon as I open the door to find Noah looking incredibly hot in a pair of black jeans and a vintage tuxedo jacket, Scruffles sticks his snout right in Noah's crotch.

"Scruffles, stop it! That's *so rude*!" I shout.

Noah manages to deflect Scruffles' interest with a gentle push and hands me a single, perfect, pink tea rose.

"They didn't come in hot pink, so this is the best I could do," he says.

"It's okay," I assure him. "This is beautiful." I hold the flower to my nose, which is enveloped by velvet petals and fragrance. "And it smells glorious." Then I carefully tuck the rose into my hair.

Noah grins in approval and says, "You look pretty amazing yourself."

"So do you," I say, feeling my cheeks flush.

I usher him into the front hall, and Scruffles follows like a shadow, tail wagging in excitement.

"You have to promise not to hold me responsible for anything my family says, okay?" I tell him. "You're about to step on deck with a bunch of loose cannons."

"Relax, Sammy," Noah says. "I didn't just emerge full formed from the primordial slime. I, too, have family members. And they are also prone to saying embarrassing things at inopportune moments."

I throw him a skeptical glance. "Trust me, you don't know embarrassing until you've met my family."

"Maybe we should have invited my parents over," Noah says, his eyes alight with amusement. "We could have had an Embarrass-Off."

"Ugh, no! I concede!" I say, and I lead him into the family room for pictures and close familial scrutiny.

"Mom, Dad, Grandma, Grandpa, RJ, this is Noah Woods. Noah, these are my parents, my grandparents, and my brother, RJ."

"Nice to meet you, young man," Grandpa says, getting up to shake Noah's hand. "Like your tux. Although in my day, we wore them with the pants, too."

And here we go . . .

"Grandpa, it's a Faux Prom. For the class outcasts," I explain for what must be the fifth time. "So we're not doing things the traditional way."

"Oh. Eh, I still don't understand why a bright kid like you would be an outcast in the first place," Grandpa says. "When I was in high school—"

"Dad, just say 'Get off my lawn' and be done with it," Mom says. "Put the poor kids out of their misery."

"My husband's actually quite lovely when you get to know him," Grandma Sally tells Noah. "Even if he seems like a strange old codger on first meeting."

"I'm Samantha's father," Dad says, going in for the handshake.

"I know," Noah says, grasping Dad's hand. "I've seen your picture in the paper."

And cue most awkward moment ever.

Noah, realizing what he's done, turns bright red. "Oh. I'm sorry. I . . . uh . . ." he stammers.

"Relax, it's not exactly a secret that I've become rather *newsworthy* in the last month or so," Dad says.

This doesn't appear to relax Noah at all. It's so awkward. I want to take his hand and run out of here before any other mortifying incidents occur.

"Can we just take the pictures?" I say. "We've got a prom to get to."

Dad gets the camera and we go to the garden. Mom directs from a chair on the patio. She and Grandma argue for five minutes over which shrub makes the best backdrop, until I remind them that we would like to get to BethAnn's house sometime tonight. They finally compromise on the rhododendron, which is heavy with fat white blossoms. They decide that will set off the pink of my dress to perfection.

"Whatever," I mutter to Noah. "Can we just take the pictures?"

"Okay," Dad says. "Say *fromage*."

We both smile and after Dad takes the first picture, I whisper to Noah, "See, we can't even just say *cheese* like normal people!"

Grandma, Mom, and Grandpa keep suggesting different poses until my cheeks hurt from smiling.

"We've got enough now," I say. "Otherwise the party is going to be over by the time we get there."

"One more," Mom says. "Noah, can you take a picture of us? The whole family?"

I'm about to complain, when I see Grandma put her arm around Mom and help her walk toward the rhododendron. Touching my great-grandmother's pearls that nestle around my neck, I say, "How about two more pictures? First, just me with Mom and Grandma."

It's worth it just for the smiles that light up Mom and Grandma's faces.

After Noah takes a full family shot, Noah and I finally get clearance to leave. Dad walks us to the door and just in case I haven't reached peak mortification already, he gives us both a short lecture about underage drinking, drinking and driving, and not making stupid mistakes.

That's when I cut him off.

"Dad, *please*. Don't you think I've learned enough about not making stupid mistakes in the last month? Can't I just go have fun tonight?"

Dad looks shocked and I'm afraid he's angry because I've crossed some invisible line. But then he laughs and gives us a rueful smile.

"I'm turning into Grandpa Marty!" he says. "Go on, you two. *Get off my lawn* and have a good time."

"You're so weird," I tell him. "Lovable, but weird."

BethAnn and her parents have decorated the shrubs around their front door with white fairy lights, so it looks like we're walking into a magical bower rather than a gathering of high school prom misfits.

Omar has brought over speakers and he's set up a DJ app on his laptop. He picks from our playlists and gives shout-outs to everyone whose list he's playing from. It turns out there are more pariahs than we thought. Out of a junior class of 641, there are 34 of us here instead of at the official prom.

After downing some food, Noah and I join the crew on the makeshift dance floor. Omar plays one from my playlist, an Einstein's Encounter slow song: "I'm Free Then." I grin at the lyrics. "I'm free then keep these chains off, show me something that I can believe in, I know what to do right now, believing in you I finally put it all behind me . . ."

"Shout out to Sammy Wallach for this romantic ballad by Einstein's Encounter," Omar says. "Otherwise known as 'the band it's worth getting grounded for.' There's a strict prohibition on ruining Sammy's enjoyment of this song by barfing on her," he adds. "*After* the song is over, however, it's fair game."

"NO!" I laugh. "No barfing on me allowed, period!"

"Don't worry," Noah assures me. "As your date, I view it as my duty to fight off all barfers."

"My knight in a mismatched tux." I sigh, batting my eyelashes in exaggerated swooniness.

"Your grandpa seemed extremely perturbed by my lack of matching pants," Noah says.

"Grandpa Marty's okay. He just doesn't get the whole Faux Prom concept."

Over Noah's shoulder I spot a new couple joining the party. My heart leaps as I see them outlined in shadow—it looks like her, but I can't be sure until they step out of the house into the light.

I pull back from Noah's arms. "Rosa's here! I can't believe she came!"

"I can," he says.

"You knew?" I ask.

He smiles, sphinxlike. "I might have had some inkling."

I throw my arms around his neck and kiss his cheek. I spin away to run across the lawn to Rosa, but he grabs my hand and pulls me back. I twirl into him and find myself staring into his eyes. "Hey," he says softly.

"Hey," I reply. Then Noah lowers his head, closing the distance between our "Heys." His lips are warm and urgent against mine, his arms a circle around me, pulling me closer. My fingers tangle in his hair, and flutters take off in my chest. Right now, in this moment, all I feel is wonder.

When he pulls back, he smiles and says, "Go on," because he knows. I grin and take off across the lawn, almost knocking Rosa over with the force of my bear hug.

"I'm so glad you're here!" I practically shout.

"When I imagined going to prom, you were always part of it," Rosa says. "We went to the actual prom and took pictures, but I knew that *real* 'real prom' was here."

"Prom is where your friends are," I say.

"Exactly," Rosa agrees. "I made a playlist. Eddy did, too."

She goes over to Omar and hands him a thumb drive.

Then, grabbing Eddy's hand, she meets Noah and me and we're all together dancing when Omar starts playing Queen's "You're My Best Friend."

Everyone ends up dancing together, spinning and singing at the top of their lungs.

The fairy lights hanging around the patio twinkle along with the stars that surround the moon shining down on us from the indigo sky.

This is a perfect moment.

And better yet—no one throws up on me to ruin it.

I've got this moment of pure joy for the hard days ahead.

My mom has two more rounds of chemo to get through. We still have to see how the cancer responds. The probability is good that it will, but you never know. My dad's future as CEO of New Territories Bank Corp is up in the air.

I still have to take the SAT next weekend. In the fall I'll be applying to college.

But tonight I'm here with my friends and one very adorable boy, and there is music, and for these few hours, in this time and place, all is right in my world.

I'll take it.

Someone else can post pictures on Instagram or Facebook or wherever to capture the memories tonight.

I'm too busy making them.

acknowledgments

A writer spends a lot of time creating alone, but the book that comes out with her name on the spine couldn't happen without the assistance of others.

First, I have to thank my amazing editor, Jody Corbett, who shepherded a grieving and emotionally fragile yours truly through the writing of this book. Somehow, she knew exactly when to push and when to allow me a day or two to be weepy. I consider myself truly blessed to work with her.

I'm grateful to work with a rock-star agent, Jennifer Laughran, who helps keep me sane in a business that is often far from it.

I'm so happy to be part of the Scholastic family, where I get to work with fun, funny, and incredibly talented people like Rebekah Wallin, Nina Goffi, Saraciea Fennell, David Levithan, Tracey van Straaten, Lizette Serrano, Emily Heddleson, Antonio Gonzalez, Michelle Campbell, Johnny Yotnakparian, Nikki Mutch, Robin Bailey Hoffman, Anna Swenson, Ann Marie Wong, and so many others who care deeply about literacy and getting quality books into the hands of young people.

Writing can be a lonely, crazy-making business, and it helps to have friends who understand. I've met writers who give me advice, support, and necessary perspective with love and humor at Kindling Words, Swinger of Birches, and in the

Sisterhood of the Brass Necklace. Huge smooches and hugs to you all.

Felicia Korengel and Carol Burney Lewis are brave, honest warriors who shared the nitty-gritty of their fight with breast cancer. Thank you for helping me get the details right. Any mistakes are mine.

Thanks go to Ted Gilman, Education Specialist and Senior Naturalist at Audubon Greenwich for helping to refresh my memory as to what flora and bird life would be present during a walk in the woods in April when I was on a tight deadline in October.

Ageless and ever-hip Robert Mizaki and Paola Muggia kept me *au courant* with the Bowery Ballroom bathroom paper towel situation. Details matter, people! I've been to my fair share of concerts in New York City, but they have me beat despite having lived there far less time.

I'm immensely grateful to Daniel A. Schwartz, Esq., of Shipman and Goodwin for answering an employment law question while on a cross-country flight, and his colleague, Ross H. Garber, Esq., for referring me. Not everyone will give hypothetical legal advice to a fictional character at the drop of a hat when an author is on a tight deadline, but these gentlemen definitely came through!

I am thankful for family and friends, near and far, who showered my family with love and wrote to us with memories of our parents. It brought courage and comfort, and gave me the strength to keep writing through grief, as Mom would have wanted.

Most of all, I'm grateful for my family. I miss my parents every single day but am so incredibly fortunate to have had their love and guidance. I've weathered their loss with my siblings, John and Anne Darer, and together we're making it through.

I am thankful every day for my incredible children, Josh and Amie, who make me laugh, inspire me, and fill me with pride.

And finally, thanks to my love, Hank Eskin, who keeps me grounded, helps find my logic flaws in probability charts and in life, and who convinced me to believe in Happily Ever After again.

about the author

Sarah Darer Littman is the critically acclaimed author of *Backlash*; *Want to Go Private?*; *Life, After*; *Purge*; and *Confessions of a Closet Catholic*, winner of the Sydney Taylor Book Award. When she's not writing novels, Sarah is an award-winning columnist for the online site CT News Junkie. She teaches creative writing as an adjunct professor in the MFA program at Western Connecticut State University and with Writopia Lab. Sarah lives in Connecticut. You can visit her online at www.sarahdarerlittman.com.